She'd known they were diamonds.

"I can't accept this bracelet," Meredith said. "It's too expensive."

"Your father gave you diamonds."

"That's different." Her heart cracked a little. Didn't he understand that diamonds were a gift of love, of engagement?

Sutter paced the narrow space. "Do what you want with the damned thing. I swear, a man can't even give you a simple birthday gift anymore."

"I don't want diamonds." She placed the gift on the table.

"Do you know what you want? Do you?" he demanded when she didn't answer.

An imp of mischief with no care for survival prompted her to say, "Yes. I'll take you."

Dear Reader,

Welcome to Silhouette **Special Edition** . . . welcome to romance. Each month, Silhouette **Special Edition** publishes six novels with you in mind—stories of love and life, tales that you can identify with—romance with that little "something special" added in.

July is a wonderful month—full of sizzling stories packed with emotion. Don't miss Debbie Macomber's warm and witty *Bride on the Loose*—the concluding tale of her series, THOSE MANNING MEN. And *Heartbreak Hank* is also in store for you—Myrna Temte's third COWBOY COUNTRY tale. Starting this month, as well, is Linda Lael Miller's new duo BEYOND THE THRESHOLD. The initial book is entitled *There and Now.*

Rounding out this month are more stories by some of your favorite authors: Bevlyn Marshall, Victoria Pade and Laurie Paige.

In each Silhouette **Special Edition** novel, we're dedicated to bringing you the romances that you dream about— stories that will delight as well as bring a tear to the eye. For me, good romance novels have always contained an element of hope, of optimism that life can be, and often is, very beautiful. I find a great deal of inspiration in that thought.

Why do you read romances? I'd really like to hear your opinions on the books that we publish and on the romance genre in general. Please write to me c/o Silhouette Books, 300 East 42nd Street, 6th floor, New York, NY 10017.

I hope that you enjoy this book and all of the stories to come. Looking forward to hearing from you!

Sincerely,

Tara Gavin
Senior Editor
Silhouette Books

LAURIE PAIGE
Man Without a Past

Silhouette Special Edition

Published by Silhouette Books New York

America's Publisher of Contemporary Romance

SILHOUETTE BOOKS
300 East 42nd St., New York, N.Y. 10017

MAN WITHOUT A PAST

ISBN: 0-373-09755-7

First Silhouette Books printing July 1992

Printed in the U.S.A.

Books by Laurie Paige

Silhouette Special Edition

Lover's Choice #170
Man Without a Past #755

Silhouette Desire

Gypsy Enchantment #123
Journey to Desire #195
Misty Splendor #304
Golden Promise #404

Silhouette Romance

South of the Sun #296
A Tangle of Rainbows #333
A Season for Butterflies #364
Nothing Lost #382
The Sea at Dawn #398
A Season for Homecoming #727
Home Fires Burning Bright #733
Man from the North Country #772

LAURIE PAIGE

has recently moved to California, where she is busy writing and falling off mountains—translation: trying to snow ski. During the summer she and her husband went camping, and she did a lot of falling there, too. Friends had brought along a sailboard, and she had to try it. As soon as she recovers from all this fun, she plans to use the information gained for some spunky heroine (who will be able to do each of them flawlessly on the second try!).

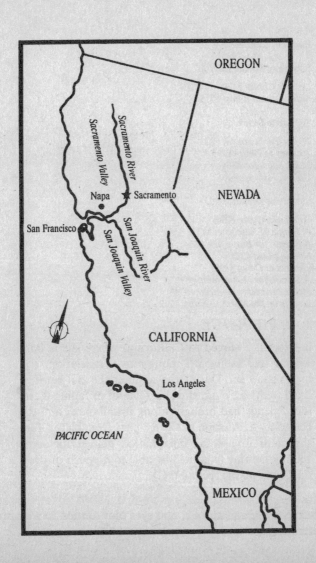

Chapter One

Meredith Lawton's mind was on marriage as she parked her ancient, but trusty, compact car beside an expensive sporty model in the guest parking space next to her father's town house. Her thoughts stirred memories better left undisturbed, but she was considering the bonds of matrimony for her father, not herself.

Her mother had died several years ago, and Meredith had decided her father should have someone to pal around with now that he was retired. Even a former workaholic scientist-engineer needed companionship and a warm body on cold, lonely nights. Meredith had someone in mind for him....

Unexpectedly, a face appeared in her inner vision, a masculine face with a classic chin, thin nose and broad forehead framed by thick black hair, lips that were firm but sensitive and mobile, and eyes that seemed to see into eternity.

Sutter's eyes…dark blue and black-lashed…sultry, sexy, moody, angry, tender—*No, angry, remember them that way.*…

She clenched her hand on the steering wheel as old-but-not-forgotten yearning suddenly washed over her, striking when she was least prepared for it. The brightness of the morning faded, and for a second she sat there, staring into space, lost in a matrix of adolescent dreams and adult reality.

An ache crept through her, similar to the emotional upheavals she'd experienced as a teenager when she'd flamed with feelings so intense they'd burned all the way to her soul. She'd been wounded and vulnerable when she'd met Sutter shortly after her mother's death, a time when she and her father had withdrawn from one another, each fighting the pain of loss alone.

Somehow Sutter had seen beyond her brash defiance to the angry, hurt young person she'd hidden inside. The fact that she hadn't become a juvenile delinquent she attributed directly to him. It had been his sympathy and advice that had helped her through the pitfalls of those days. She'd cried out her despair in his arms.

Sutter's arms. Meredith had never forgotten their strength and warmth, how sweetly he'd held her in her grief. Years later he'd held her again, heart pressed to heart, not in grief that time, but in passion.

Meredith climbed out of her car, anxious to escape those particular memories, and glanced at the other vehicles in the parking area. Sutter's old pickup with the camper shell wasn't in sight.

Exhaling in relief, she admitted she didn't like being taken by surprise. She'd seen more of Sutter since her father's heart attack three months ago than in the past three years. Being around him so much bothered her.

Frowning over this admission, she hurried across the lawn. The door to the town house was open. She bounded up the three steps and went in without knocking.

"Anybody home?" she yelled.

"I'm in the office," Richard Lawton yelled back.

"Naturally," she muttered to herself with a smile.

She leaped down from the raised parquet floor of the entrance, her sneakers landing silently on the carpet, and went down the hallway to the back of the town house.

"You're supposed to be getting ready for our vacation," she scolded, sticking her head around the door frame. "Oh."

Eyes, deeply blue and black-lashed, an amused glint in their depths, met her startled gaze. Her heart whirred in her chest like a startled pheasant.

"Hello, Mary, Mary, quite contrary," Sutter Kinnard said, a trace of Alabama accent still discernible in his voice after eleven years of living in California.

She saw him take in her hair, swept back into a ponytail, her face, bare of makeup, the T-shirt that hugged her torso, the old pair of shorts, ragged at the hem, and finally her legs and the knee socks scrunched around her ankles. Anger jolted through her. She resented his catching her by surprise, his seeing her in ratty clothes and, most of all, his greeting.

Sutter had teased her with the old nursery rhyme the first time her father had brought the young man to their house. She'd been fourteen, and Sutter had been twenty-two, newly graduated from Auburn University and starting his first job as an engineer in Silicon Valley. He'd worked for her father in those days, but now he owned his own company.

"Hello, Mary, Mary," he'd said all those years ago, making up his own nickname for her. "How's the garden?'' Not very original, but his voice had been heavenly. And he'd smiled at her so sweetly. She'd loved him from the first instant. *Eleven years ago . . .*

She shook off the memory. She was almost twenty-five now, definitely not the child who'd thought Sutter was her personal Prince Charming. She'd learned better three years ago when he'd briefly succumbed to the passion she'd felt for him for years.

''The drive from Sacramento must have been bad. She's still in shock,'' Sutter said to her father when she failed to reply.

He wore a blue polo shirt and old jeans that clung to his lean hips as if custom-made for him. He looked healthy and fit, not at all the way a harried executive should look.

She recovered her poise and arched her brows at him. ''The shock is from seeing you. What's the great entrepreneur doing here? I assumed you never left the offices of CNI, especially since the *big move.*''

CNI stood for Communications Networks, Incorporated. He'd started the business five years ago. Recently the company had moved into new quarters near Sacramento.

Her turf, she thought, and the resentment flared again. He had no right moving to her territory. Her lips tightened, and she had to force the smile back on her face.

The men exchanged glances. Sutter made a gesture indicating her father should go first. She tensed, waiting for bad news.

''We're just going over a couple of things,'' Dr. Lawton said, waving his hand as if that explained everything.

Meredith narrowed her eyes as suspicion darted through her. She looked pointedly at her father. ''We're supposed to leave for vacation tomorrow. Remember?''

"Certainly," her father assured her. "I thought I'd take a few, uh, charts with me. I'm cleaning up the forty meg now and copying some files I'll need for the laptop."

"You're retired. You're supposed to be goofing off." She settled her hands on her hips in exasperation. "What are you working on now?"

He had the grace to look a tiny bit guilty. "Well, nothing much, just an idea or two." He eyed her old shorts and faded T-shirt from the National Zoo, a relic of a long-past vacation. "Are you going to clean out the refrigerator?" he asked with a hopeful gleam appearing in his hazel green eyes.

She was acutely aware of Sutter's gaze running over her as she pretended to let herself be distracted by her father's evasive tactics. She'd get to the bottom of this little mystery before the day was over.

Ignoring Sutter's intent study as best she could, she spoke to her father. "Why else would I get up at dawn on a perfectly wonderful day in June—"

"Is it June already?"

Meredith laughed and relaxed somewhat. Her father was constantly amazed at the passage of time, as if the days sneaked by when he wasn't looking, tricking him. Sometimes she felt the same, only with an increasing loneliness. Hence her quest to find him a companion. One of them should be happy.

She shoved the thought into the background. Approaching the quarter-century mark certainly made a person morbid.

"June the first," she told him and continued her complaint, "I was on the road before ten, I'll have you know. I expect to be home before dark."

She reminded him of their plans to spend a month cruising around the Sacramento delta country on a houseboat supplied by the state of California. Actually, it would be a working vacation for her. She had a contract for a water study.

She glanced at Sutter when he stirred and recrossed his legs at the ankles. He lounged in a straight-backed chair, filling the room with a force field of power and male presence that dwarfed her father, who was not a small man.

Sutter shifted at the flow of energy that rushed through his body. It was almost like a spurt of adrenaline, preparing him to run or fight...or make love. He shifted again, restless and tense with sensations he didn't want to acknowledge. And with a reaction he didn't want anyone else in the room to notice.

Meredith's voice flowed on, scolding her father in her saucy way that wasn't in the least offensive. She wasn't a nagging female, but neither was she shy about letting a male in on his shortcomings. Once she'd lectured him about life and housekeeping and things like that. Those days were long gone.

He suddenly wished they could go back to that time of purity and innocence, when she'd looked at him with her eyes shining in happiness with some new idea she had. She'd been so sweet.

"It's almost time for lunch."

Richard's voice broke into his reverie as the scientist peered at the clock on his desk. He gave his daughter another hopeful look, then smiled as she heaved a sigh.

"I'll check the refrigerator," she said.

From his vantage point, Sutter watched her walk down the hall and disappear into the kitchen. She was much like the long-legged teenager he'd met years ago. Except she was all woman now. And that fact disturbed the hell out of him.

He wished he could tousle her bangs like he used to and she'd pretend to get mad and they'd end up in a friendly fight....

A picture of her under him, her hair fanned out over the sofa cushion, a dark tangle with fiery highlights, came to him. Her eyes—neither green nor brown, but some of both—watched him, glowing with passion, filled with trust.

Remorse stabbed his conscience. He'd nearly betrayed that trust. Worst of all, he wanted her now, *right this moment,* with a hard, aching need that made him furious with himself.

He noticed Richard looking at him expectantly. "I'm sorry. What did you say?"

They discussed the new bid CNI was preparing.

In the kitchen, Meredith found the coffeemaker still on, the pot empty. She flicked it off and surveyed the contents of the refrigerator. If she kept busy, she decided, she wouldn't have to think. She realized how ridiculous that sounded.

Sutter's presence had disturbed her emotional equilibrium. She'd thought she had finally learned to maintain an outward calm around him.

She hooked a strand of hair behind her ear and realized her fingers were cold and shaky. "Damn," she said.

"What's wrong?" Sutter asked, coming into the kitchen and peering over her shoulder. "Nothing to eat?"

Standing so close behind her that she could feel his body heat, he was a force impossible to ignore. Whether close or across the room, she'd never been able to overlook him, she admitted.

"I think there's some sandwich stuff." She lifted a package from the meat drawer. "Um-hmm. Would you prefer the green fuzzy ham or the gray fuzzy cheese?"

He chuckled. "Sounds like the choices at my place."

His breath caressed the side of her neck, causing a chill to march down one arm. She moved aside. "Have you run off your housekeeper, too?"

"What makes you think I have one?" he quipped, reaching both arms around her to lift a bowl, remove the plastic cover and peer at the contents.

"Don't you?" Meredith shivered delicately at the moldy remains of a casserole she'd prepared a week ago.

"I have a cleaning service twice a week; otherwise I manage on my own. Fortunately, I had a friend who lectured me on proper housekeeping procedures years ago."

She leaned her head sideways to look at him, her mouth only inches from his. His perusal was tender with memories. There was also a question in those sea blue depths, as if he could see the turmoil in her soul and wondered at it.

For a second, she was seized by the wild impulse to turn into his arms and kiss him until neither of them could stand.

Sutter noted the darkening of Meredith's eyes, caused by the widening of her pupils, and the way her lashes lowered to that sexy, slumberous invitation a woman issued when she wanted a man. Every nerve in his body tightened to the snapping point.

He clenched his teeth against a groan and warned his imagination to back off. Lately, she seemed more likely to hate him than to want him.

She turned away just as he shifted forward to press his length against hers, a move that was entirely subconscious until he'd already started the motion and then realized what he was doing. She smelled of shampoo and sunshine and pure essence of woman, a combination he found irresistible. He stepped back.

"I'll make a tuna salad," she decided, ducking under his arm to inspect the cupboards. "Then I'll throw the other stuff out before the health department declares the fridge a hazardous waste zone." She put the bowl in the sink.

"I'll help," he volunteered, wondering why he was letting himself in for this torture and why they couldn't be easy around each other anymore. He'd hoped they'd finally recovered from that disastrous night three years ago when he'd let passion overrule his brain. In fact, he'd thought her father's illness had put them back on the path of their old tried-and-true friendship, but the last couple of encounters had proved him wrong.

He reached past her into the open cupboard and retrieved a fairly fresh loaf of bread. His forearm brushed the sensitive skin under her upper arm before he withdrew and went to the toaster. She glanced at him and just as swiftly looked away.

Passion was the problem. It was between them at this moment, he acknowledged, a thorn that pricked and tormented until he wanted to brush his lips against the soft nape of her neck and feel her quicken beneath his hands as she'd once done.

A tingle passed through his fingers. She'd been so warmly responsive to his touch, her skin so soft, her body pliable under his, giving him whatever he wanted—

Damn! He was doing it again, remembering things that were better forgotten. He wanted to return to those uncomplicated early days, when she'd been a child on the brink of growing up. They'd been the happiest of his life.

Richard Lawton and his daughter had accepted him into their home and their lives. They'd made him feel welcome. They'd let him be a part of their family, a real family. He'd never betray that trust.

Sutter's arm grazed Meredith's once more while they worked side by side in the narrow kitchen. They'd fixed meals like this often over the years, Meredith recalled. In those early days, she'd assumed he'd fall in love with her and they'd marry when she finished school. It had seemed inevitable.

Just a moment ago, she'd seen a trace of deeper emotion in his eyes, but it was gone in an instant and he'd returned to his usual manner toward her—sardonic and teasing.

Lately, she'd started to feel stifled around Sutter. For years, they'd held to the pretense that she was the adolescent he'd first met, not the woman she'd become. She was tired of the act, she realized, plopping the mayonnaise jar down on the tiled counter with unintentional force.

"Easy," Sutter cautioned. He gave her ponytail a tug. "Who's tweaked your temper today?"

She turned on him, needing to vent her frustration. "What's going on between you and my father?" she asked in a low tone.

"Nothing clandestine," Sutter replied, a wary smile lifting the corners of his mouth.

She wasn't amused. "He's only been out of the hospital a little over three months."

A curtain descended over Sutter's eyes, making her more and more certain of a plot between the two men.

"He's going to do some work for me. For CNI."

"He's not," she denied, keeping her voice soft so her father wouldn't hear, but speaking vehemently nevertheless.

"Yes."

"Dammit, Sutter, he's supposed to be taking it easy, not getting involved with your projects! He had a heart attack!"

He laid a finger over her lips. Tingles cascaded all the way down her throat to her breasts. Her nipples contracted with sudden painful force, and she crossed her arms defensively.

But not before he'd noticed. His gaze flicked down, then back to her face. A moment of awareness hung suspended between them, a single instant too fragile to bridge the distance he'd placed between them three years ago when he'd rejected her love.

"Did you find anything?" her father asked, appearing at the kitchen door. She and Sutter moved apart.

The tension eased, but she gave Sutter a glance that said the discussion wasn't over, not by a long shot! She turned with a smile to her father. "Your favorite, tuna salad."

He groaned in response to her teasing. In her younger days, tuna salad had figured heavily in her meal plans.

"Is it about ready? I have to pack my clothes—"

"You'll only need a few things, Dad," she assured him. "Throw in a couple of bathing suits, some T-shirts, shorts, a pair of jeans and a windbreaker. That should do it."

Sutter removed toast slices and inserted more bread into the toaster. "Won't you need dress clothes for dinner? Or are you going to cook for a solid month?"

Dr. Lawton laughed at the question. "Meredith is as forgetful of meals as I am."

"I know," Sutter said, smiling at her, his eyes becoming warm with a hundred shared memories of their past.

Meredith slapped tuna salad on toast. "There are lots of places to eat along the way. We'll stop often," she promised her father. "Besides, the plan was to have fresh fish several nights a week, if I recall correctly."

She prodded Dr. Lawton with an elbow, reminding him that he was supposed to fish and relax while she worked.

When the sandwiches were ready, Sutter opened their drinks, cola for her, beer for him and Dr. Lawton. They went to the table on the sunny deck to eat.

"Wish I could go cruising up and down a river," he said.

He actually sounded wistful, she noted. "It's all in knowing the right people." She smiled as if she had secrets she had no intention of sharing.

"Richard said the water study you did for the city got you the new one with the state. Tell me about it," he invited.

As a specialist in water quality, Meredith found her talents much in demand as a water shortage plagued the entire western United States. She explained her new contract, which involved collecting water samples and recording temperatures at various points along the thousand miles of river channel and canals that formed the Sacramento delta. At the university in Sacramento, she'd spend the next year analyzing the samples and writing a paper on the findings. Two graduate students had been assigned to her.

"That's damned impressive," Sutter admitted when she finished. "You're making a name for yourself as an expert."

"My next project is already in the works, a job for the National Park Service, studying western rivers. I'm keeping notes on all my research so I can write a book on the subject."

"You could do two books," he suggested. "One for your fellow hydrologists, another for the general public."

"I hadn't considered that." She stared into the distance as she thought it over. "I could alert the public to the problems, give them some idea of the solutions being considered and some suggestions on how they could help.

But," she added with a sigh, "I have to finish my doctoral dissertation first."

She caught Sutter's smile of satisfaction as he lifted the can to his lips. He had successfully taken her mind off the worry over her father and was pleased with himself.

He thought he knew her so well. He'd once declared, in the midst of an argument over some small event, that he knew her better than she knew herself; after all, he'd helped raise her through her rebellious stage.

But he didn't, she realized with sudden insight. From the time she was fourteen until she was twenty-two, Sutter had been her very best friend. At twenty-two, she'd been ready to cross the threshold from friend to lover. He hadn't. In the three years since, she'd avoided him if possible. Until her father's illness three months ago had thrown them together again in common concern.

Sutter, she mused, had loved her as a child, but not as a woman. Sudden tears stung her eyes.

"So, what's this about working for CNI?" she asked, returning to her earlier concern.

After a pause, Sutter answered, "Your dad's going to do some consulting work for us—"

"Just checking over ideas to see if they're feasible," Dr. Lawton interrupted, his expression eager.

"And looking over designs for any obvious errors," Sutter added before taking a big bite out of his sandwich.

"I see," Meredith said.

She mulled it over while she ate. Realizing there was nothing she could do—her father was a grown man and she wasn't his keeper—she accepted his working as a fait accompli.

"I assume the work is in progress. How do you plan on communicating while we're on the river?" she asked.

Sutter wiped his mouth and laid the napkin aside. "CNI will supply a cellular phone. When I know where you're tying up for the night, I'll drive down and go over any problems."

"You'll be coming to the houseboat?" She was unable to hide her dismay and hoped it sounded as if she were anxious on her father's account only.

"It's going to work out perfectly," Dr. Lawton said happily.

"We won't always be stopping near a road," she told the two men, returning Sutter's steady perusal with one of her own. An unspoken challenge leaped to life between them.

After lunch, when Sutter had left and her father had returned to his office, she began tossing out the food that had accumulated since the last housekeeper had quit. The woman had lasted six months before making the fatal mistake of cleaning Dr. Lawton's office. By emptying the trash, she'd tossed out several pages of calculations he'd decided he needed. The woman had left after an exchange of heated words.

Meredith shook her head. The incident was a classic example of why her father needed a helpmate. Not a caretaker. Oh, no, he couldn't stand to be "looked after" as if he were a kid, but he did need some helpful reminders on occasion.

A wife was the answer, someone who would love him and accept his quirks of character just as he would accept hers. And Meredith had the perfect woman for him.

The satisfied grin left her mouth as her thoughts skittered once more toward the rough terrain of old memories.

The month of June was a hard one for her heart. It had been so since that disastrous night of passion three years ago. This summer didn't appear any different. On Friday the fourteenth, only thirteen days away, she'd be twenty-five.

A quarter of a century. Not so long, and yet . . . forever.

The birthday she didn't want to remember had been her twenty-second one. She'd been fresh out of college and very much in love. She suddenly felt sorry for that girl who'd thought the world revolved around her dreams. She'd learned better.

"The hard way," she murmured with a sigh.

Clamping a lid on the useless thoughts, Meredith made up a cleaning solution to wash the inside of the refrigerator after grinding the leftovers down the disposal. From the back of the town house, the whir of the vacuum cleaner drowned out her dismal thoughts.

Her father was actually quite nicely domesticated . . . once he turned his attention to the tasks at hand. He vacuumed while she finished the refrigerator. Then she dusted while he washed a load of clothes and decided what to pack for their month of cruising.

Meredith had been amazed to learn the houseboat was part of her contract. She had no idea what it looked like, but had a secret dread it might be some old wreck donated to the state and written off as a tax deduction.

Ah, well, she'd learned to handle life's difficult moments. Just the thought of being on the river was exciting. All she asked for was a chance to do her work and relax.

As evening approached, she again reminded Dr. Lawton they needed to drive to her place in order to get off to an early start in the morning. He packed his clothing.

"Ready to go?" she asked, hooking stray wisps of hair behind her ears when he returned to the office.

Dr. Lawton cast an uneasy gaze around the desk. She followed his glance. Everything was neat.

"Sutter said he'd be back with some drawings before we left," he finally admitted. "I might need to bring a book.... What did I do with that text on micro...?" The rest of the sentence was lost as he rooted among the crowded bookshelves.

Meredith frowned in exasperation. Before she could speak, a knock sounded on the front door.

"That must be him," her father said in relief. He went to the door. "Come on in."

"Sorry to be so late. I got tied up in a meeting." Sutter's dark blue gaze flicked to her. "Trouble?"

Meredith couldn't hide her displeasure. "We were supposed to spend the night at my apartment so we could get an early start. You could have dropped the stuff off there and saved another long trip."

Sutter had avoided her place after that one visit. Who could blame him? It had been there that she'd handed her heart—and her body—to him on a platter. He'd politely handed both of them right back.

But not until he'd kissed her as if there'd be no tomorrow and had touched her....

She'd never been able to forget. It had been all her dreams come true. The setting had been perfect. A cool night in June, rain billowing across the road in windswept sheets like gauze curtains, unusual for California in the summer.

"Well, we need to go over a few things first." Her father broke into her stormy thoughts. "Then I want to check out a few calculations against the earlier ones Sutter gave me."

"I think I'll sit on the deck for a while," she said abruptly. Leaving the office, she walked out on the wooden deck and braced her weight against her arms, letting her anger cool.

The coastal fog drifted along the tops of the hills that separated the valley from the ocean. At low places in the ridges, the mist rolled downward, tumbling over itself in its eagerness to reach some hidden point, some secret rendezvous only it knew.

An ache started inside, and she pressed a hand to her heart. Enough, she ordered her restless spirit; she was tired of memories. She sank into the hanging basket chair and set it to swinging.

She closed her eyes and let her mind grow whimsical. While they were eating, her father had asked what she wanted for her birthday this year. "What every woman wants," she'd joked, "jewels, trips around the world, things like that."

What she really wanted couldn't be put into words. A man whose love she could trust. A commitment to their future through marriage and children. A partner who'd share life and love as equals. Little things like that.

"Ready to go?"

She turned the swinging basket chair so she could look at Sutter. He stood with his back to the door, the light behind him.

An image came to her—one of Sutter encapsulated in an ice crystal, so cold and self-contained that no one, especially not her, could penetrate it. Sometimes she could almost hate him for that cool aloofness. He never needed anyone.

"You can ride back to Sacramento with me," he said. "I want to talk to you. Your father can drive your car over early in the morning. He's not ready to leave."

"He would have been if you'd left him alone," she snapped.

She stood and folded her arms across her torso as goose bumps raced along her skin. The night was typically cold when the sun went down. Since she'd planned on being home before that event, she'd brought no warm clothing with her.

"He's ordered a pizza for dinner. We can stop on the way to Sacramento and eat," Sutter continued, overlooking her outburst. His eyes narrrowed. "Didn't you bring any clothes with you?"

"Only what I have on."

"I have a jacket in the car."

It seemed the trip was planned. To protest further would make too much of the event. Besides, it didn't bother her to be in his company. That is, usually she could control her emotions and pretend to be as carefree as the young girl she'd once been. Today was unusually difficult for some reason.

"I'll say good-night to Dad, then we can go."

She went inside, Sutter at her heels like an alert guard, and kissed her father on the cheek. His mind was already locked into his work, she saw.

"See you in the morning," she told him. "I'll send out the national guard if you're not at my place by eight."

"I'll be there."

"Okay," she said, then turned to Sutter. "Let's go."

Sutter's tight-lipped smile warned her of the conversation to come. She wasn't in the mood for a lecture, but she followed him out without protest. They had miles in which to argue.

He opened the door to the new sports car she'd seen earlier and closed it when she was inside. After he was in, he reached behind his seat and pulled out a nylon jacket, which he tossed to her. The scent of his cologne surrounded her when she draped it over her. Sadness folded around her as softly as the nylon.

She was silent while he maneuvered into traffic on the street and then the interstate. He turned on the heat once they were on the highway and the engine had warmed up. After a while, the silence, which she'd found relaxing at first, became oppressive. The air became charged with repressed emotion. Hers or his?

"Nice car." She ran a hand over the smooth upholstery. "I'm surprised. I thought you'd never give up the old clunker."

He chuckled. "It finally died, dramatically, I might add, in the middle of a downtown intersection at rush hour. You would've enjoyed the ruckus that caused, horns blowing and people shouting for me to get out of the way."

"I can imagine."

He fell silent while they sped along the freeway. At a small town up the road, he stopped at her favorite barbecue restaurant. They ate and were on the road again in less than an hour.

Sutter was good at remembering things other people liked, Meredith recalled, feeling cynical about that facet of his personality for some reason. In fact, she felt downright contrary, which was probably overreaction to the irritation she'd felt with herself for letting him influence her mood in the first place.

Chill out, she advised herself, using slang she'd learned from the university students. Sinking into the comfort of the luxurious seat, she wearily reminded herself it had been a long day.

It wasn't over yet.

Chapter Two

"About your father," Sutter said, his voice slicing through the dark silence, low and deep and vibrant. Just the sound of it, or perhaps the subject he chose, offended her.

Her reactions were tumultuous tonight. She had to control them better. Outside the car window, the countryside whipped by at a steady sixty-five miles per hour. Cruise control, that's what she needed, a device to set her emotions on automatic and let her get on with her life.

She tried to find the thought amusing, but, sitting there beside the one man she'd once loved totally and unconditionally, she felt starkly alone. It wasn't a new feeling for her. She'd just never felt it when she was with him.

"I'm not going to cause trouble about his working," she said quietly. She heard the loneliness echo in her voice.

Sutter didn't. He shot her a surprised glance.

She shrugged. "What good would it do? He knows as well as I do that he's supposed to stay away from problems and stick to his exercise program. And *you* know he'll forget all that as soon as he gets involved on your projects."

"He needs the work," Sutter stated.

"I beg your pardon?" She knew her father didn't need money.

"He needs something to occupy his mind," Sutter clarified. "He'll die of boredom if he sits around doing nothing. Your father's a brilliant man—"

"I know that, but did you ever think *I* might have ideas about his welfare that you haven't considered?"

"Such as?" The hint of frost in his tone didn't faze her.

"Companionship and a scoop of plain, old-fashioned fun."

"Bull."

"Just the reaction I'd expect from you."

"Just the solution I'd expect from you."

"You're so good at that," she murmured.

"At what?" He was irritated and it showed.

"The absolute-zero chill factor when someone says something you don't like. You become all cold and distant, a glacier."

He cast another look of irritation her way.

"Relax," she advised. "You're choking the steering wheel."

"Yeah, and it's a poor substitute for what I'd like to choke."

"My neck?"

She took his snort as assent.

"You don't scare me, Sutter. And you're not always right."

"No?" He lifted one dark eyebrow, an elegant move she'd seen Clark Gable make many times in old movies. It was as effective when Sutter did it. He turned off the highway onto a country road that was dark and deserted, and stopped.

He twisted around in the seat to face her. "Still feeling brave?"

She swallowed the lump that had formed in her throat and nodded. She'd die before she'd beg for mercy. "I haven't a cowardly bone in my body. You told me so yourself, remember?"

"Yes. You never backed down from a fight if you believed in your cause."

"I still don't. Remember that, Mr. Tycoon."

"A threat?" he mused. "You've been spoiling for a fight since you showed up this morning. Let's have at it."

"All right," she agreed. "Why couldn't you have left my father's welfare up to me?"

"When was the last time you went to visit him?"

Meredith tried to figure out this angle of attack. "I've dropped in every weekend since he's been home. I stayed with him for a week after he got out of the hospital. You know that."

"Then you should have noticed he was restless and at loose ends. When he called me about a new contract," Sutter continued, "he wanted to know if there was anything he could do. He volunteered to act as a consultant for *free*. That should give you an idea of his desperation. A man can't work all his life, then suddenly be stuck on the shelf, no longer wanted or needed."

"He was needed," she said, mulling over the implications. "I told him about my plans. He volunteered to chart the river data on the laptop."

"Data input doesn't tax the brain. He needs more than that."

"Which I have arranged for," she contended. "I have a friend who's going to join us—"

"A woman?"

"Yes. A psychologist I met in a flower-arranging class. She's a widow, semiretired; that is, she teaches a night class at the university." Meredith stopped speaking when Sutter smiled with cynical amusement.

"That's your solution to life, isn't it, Meredith?"

She studied his face in the moonlight, not sure of his change in mood. He was as unpredictable as she found herself to be of late. He leaned closer to her and lifted a hand to her face. With one finger, he traced the outline of her lips. A tremor started deep inside her.

"You think every male needs a female to make his life perfect, don't you?"

She brushed his hand aside and glared at him, hating it when he turned superior and caustic.

"You believe in fairy tales," he scoffed. His hand dropped lightly to her shoulder. His mouth hovered only inches from hers.

"What do you believe in, Sutter?" she challenged.

His eyes narrowed until they were focused on her face, her mouth. "Not fantasies," he murmured. "The thing between male and female is . . . this."

Sutter lowered his head, taking her by surprise, catching her in the act of denial, her mouth open, vulnerable to invasion. He swept inside before she could retreat and erect defenses. His tongue found hers. For one split second, he wondered what the hell he was doing, but he didn't pull back.

The blood sizzled through his veins. It had been a long time, too damned long, since he'd tasted anything as tempting. For a moment, he couldn't resist taking a nibble of the forbidden fruit.

Desire exploded into needs he could barely control. Yearning broke through his restraint. Instead of fighting the invasion, she took the battle to him, returning every caress. He sampled the kiss in a thousand different ways while her fingers raked into his hair and held him as captive as he held her.

Even as he sensed her yielding, he fought it. For both of them. He wasn't the man for her. But she was like honey in his hands and when she flowed into him . . .

Meredith felt him hesitate with his hand on her shoulder, then he moved, both his arms enclosing her, drawing her close, breast to breast, pounding heart against pounding heart.

The kiss changed instantly. What had started out as a lesson changed in a flash point to passion. She sensed his anger, his shock, his own denial, then every thought evaporated in the moist heat of their joining.

For another second, she tasted the heady elixir of triumph. Then he wrenched her away and moved back into his seat, his arms crossed over the steering wheel, his forehead pressed to them.

"God, what a fool," he muttered.

"Well, thanks, Sutter." She was nonchalant, clinging tightly to the illusion of victory.

"Not you, me."

She let her silence speak for her and tried not to feel the hurt of his rejection.

He started the engine and returned to the highway, joining in the never-ending stream of vehicles that ferried people hither and yon on their various pursuits. Meredith curled her legs under her and said nothing. She looked at the road and ignored the glances he sent her way. He was worried about her, about hurting her feelings, and that hurt more than anything.

In the city, he didn't ask directions to her place. Although he'd been there only once, he remembered the location.

"I'll walk you to your door," he said when they arrived.

"Such a gentleman."

"Just keep quiet." He spoke without heat and sounded weary.

At the apartment, she quickly inserted the key and stepped inside. "Thanks for the ride."

"Invite me in for coffee," he said, looking past her, his eyes taking in the changes she'd made in her home in three years.

"No."

His gaze flicked back to her, crystal hard, as sharp as broken glass. "Why not?"

Other than common courtesy, she no longer worried about injuring the fragile male ego. "I don't want you here."

"Why are you so impossible these days? Since your father's illness, you seem to hold a grudge against me."

Sutter had stayed on hand during the first frightening week after her father's heart attack. He'd been the one person she'd called after arriving at the hospital, and he'd come to her. She'd slept in his arms on the waiting-room sofa.

"You were wonderful," she said with a husky catch in her voice. She touched his cheek in remembered gratitude, yearning ripping through her before she could deny it.

His skin was smooth, as if he'd shaved before returning to her father's place. She cupped her hand to the line of his jaw and explored the hardness of the bone underneath the warm flesh. That was Sutter, rock-hard in some ways, but with an overlay of warmth to temper the edges.

"I really am tired," she explained, realizing how very true that was. "Thanks for the ride. See you around."

She closed the door and snapped the lock into place. Waiting, she finally heard his footsteps on the porch. He was gone.

She leaned against the door, recalling another night, another dinner, another return to this very door....

"Come in," she'd said all those years ago, stepping through the doorway into her small apartment.

When Sutter was inside, the living room seemed even smaller. It was the first time he'd been there since she'd transferred to Sacramento for her last two years of college. She'd graduated only the week before, and the occasion was a double celebration; her birthday had also occurred during the week.

Sutter's gifts had been dinner at a fancy restaurant, flowers and candy. Her father had remembered to send her a check. It had been made out by his secretary, but he had signed it.

"Wine?" she asked Sutter. "I have burgundy or cabernet."

"Cab," he said, walking around the room and inspecting her sparse decorations and pictures.

She noted he stood for a long time before one painting—that of a city street on a rainy winter night. The street was barren, with leafless trees and empty sidewalks, but the houses had lights in the windows. She imagined all the families safe and happy inside their homes, gathered about the dinner table to share the news of their day.

When she handed him the glass of wine, he turned his gaze on her, studying her as if seeing her for the first time.

"What?" she asked, tilting her head up. At five-eleven, he stood six inches taller than she.

How could a man who was as lean and rangy as a wild steer have so much *presence?*

He gestured at the picture. "There's no people in it." He frowned. "Doesn't it make you sad?"

"Me?" Her smile proved him wrong. She was happy, deliriously so, just being with him. Shimmers of sensation ran down her back like crystal waterfalls, first hot, then cold. She glanced at the painting. "The people are inside, snug and warm." *Like her.*

To cover the jittery state of her nerves, she drank deeply of the red wine, the taste of oak and tannin lingering on her tongue. Sutter would taste like that. If they were to kiss.

She saw him glance at her lips, then away. Had her thoughts reached his? What would his mouth feel like on hers? He had the most marvelous lips and a smile that would stop the most cynical of women dead in her tracks.

Meredith knew she wasn't cynical at all.

Sutter reached over and smoothed a strand of hair at her temple. Little eddies of heat swirled down her neck and lodged in her chest. Would he touch her again?

She wanted him to. She wanted intimacy, urgent and breathless. Flustered at the wild feelings rushing through her, she turned away. "I'll light a fire," she murmured.

"I'll do it." He pushed her aside. "That's man's work, don't you know?"

"A woman can build a fire just as well as any man," she stated, immediately taking up the cudgel in defense of equality.

"Yeah," he agreed, glancing over his shoulder at her, his gaze slipping along her figure briefly before he returned his attention to the fireplace.

Before the flames flickered over the kindling, heat was already spreading through her. "I'll put some coffee on."

She set her glass down and rushed to the closet-sized kitchen just off the living room. She put coffee and water in the pot and plugged it in, then leaned against the counter.

She was twenty-two, a college graduate and, therefore, a grown woman with a capable mind. *Act like one!*

That was the problem. She was reacting to Sutter as a woman would to a dynamic, attractive man. A man she'd hero-worshiped for years.

"The fire's started." His voice interrupted her musings. "Come finish your wine."

He stood in the doorway, filling it. Meredith walked past him when he stepped back a pace to let her through. His hand touched the small of her back as they went to the two-cushion sofa before the fire. They sat side by side.

"Are you nervous?" He peered at her quizzically over the edge of his glass before he drank.

"Yes."

"Why?" He didn't seem amused by her dilemma.

She rested her head on the sofa back and stared into the licking flames. With a husky laugh directed at herself, she explained, "I've never had a man in my apartment before. Until last year, I'd always lived at home." Stupid. He knew that.

His dark brows rose a fraction, "I assumed you'd met someone you wanted to...know better. I thought that was why you moved."

"No. I just wanted to be on my own for a change. I'd always lived on the fringes of my father's life. I decided I wanted a life of my own."

"Did you find it?"

"A life of my own?"

He nodded.

Had she? She'd liked fixing up her small apartment with its cozy living room, two tiny bedrooms, kitchen and bath, all compactly arranged. After that, there had been her studies. She'd had to work hard for her grades. And she'd had friends.

She shrugged. "I suppose. I mean, I've been involved in the usual things, ball games and dances, tennis, hiking, all that."

The fire warmed her legs; his body warmed her side, all the way down. She kicked off her evening sandals and pulled her feet under her, moving away from him by leaning into the corner.

"The coffee's done. I'll get it. Sit still," he ordered.

Alone on the sofa, she wanted to cry. The tears pressed with frightening urgency behind her lids. Tension echoed along her nerves. Something portentous was going to happen....

"Here—milk and one sugar," he said, handing her a mug fixed the way she liked it. She was surprised. Women remembered things like that. Men didn't. At least, her father hadn't.

"My father doesn't even know where the kitchen is, much less how to prepare a pot of coffee. He doesn't remember whether he likes it black or not. He just accepts it the way I give it to him. I used to experiment to see if he'd notice if it had milk or sugar. Only once, after I put in three spoonfuls, did he comment that it seemed sweeter than usual."

Sutter chuckled.

An enchanting sound. She wanted to hear it again. He drained the glass of wine and set it aside. She set the mug down. They watched the fire while the rain beat against the windows. Her nerves stretched and stretched until she ached with longing.

"Meredith," he said.

She looked at him, surprised by the protest she heard in his voice. Their eyes met. His eyes were so dark, they looked black instead of blue.

He frowned. "You shouldn't look at a man that way, little girl."

Inside her, vast crevasses opened, collapsed, rose upward, sank down. Everything was in turmoil just from the way he looked at her. What would happen when he touched her?

"Give me a birthday kiss, then I've got to go," he said, reverting to his usual sardonic older-brother routine.

She licked her lips and waited, her face lifted to his. Their mouths touched, and her lips parted. She was tired of being called a little girl. She felt his surprise when she threaded her fingers through his hair.

He made a low groaning sound as his arms slid around her.

"Sutter," she whispered, her breath a whirlwind in her throat.

Then she couldn't speak. His mouth—his perfectly formed, perfectly devastating mouth—covered hers in a kiss that sizzled with the heat of their contact.

It was beautiful.

His hands caressed her arms, running up and down them before sliding into her hair and bringing her mouth harder to his. His thumbs stroked the tender flesh beneath her chin. Flames roared along the pathway of nerves in her body. She trembled with love, with the ecstasy of his touch. It was everything she'd dreamed.

She touched him. Sliding her hands over his shoulders, feeling the firmness of his flesh beneath his shirt, she marveled at the strength she discovered as his muscles flexed under her fingertips. She slipped her hands between their bodies.

He raised his head. She unfastened his tie. He yanked it off and tossed it on the floor somewhere behind them.

She laughed, giddy with the delight of being held by him at last. "Oh, Sutter," she said, filled with the need to tell him how she felt. How he felt to her. How wonderful they felt together.

He smiled slightly, then kissed her, harder this time, a man's kiss with a man's demand behind it. She linked her hands behind his neck and returned the pressure.

Her breasts flattened against his chest. She rubbed against him, wringing another deep, soft groan from him. "I've wanted you for so long. Years and years."

"You shouldn't tell a man that," he muttered.

"I can't help it."

He lifted her to his lap. The arousal in his body brought a gasp to her throat. "That's never happened so fast," he said, looking almost shocked, almost angry.

She moved closer and lifted her face again. He kissed her with little skimming touches that only whetted her appetite. When she made a throaty protest and thrust her fingers into his hair to hold him still, he muttered under his breath, but teased her more, kissing along her cheek, nibbling on her ear, refusing her his mouth until she was wild.

"Open your mouth," he ordered. "I want to taste you...have to...shouldn't..."

His muttering made no sense. Only his tantalizing caresses meant anything.

"Don't stop," she said when he drew away. She scarcely recognized her own voice, it was so husky with emotion. Passion rose in shimmering red heat waves, pulsating deep inside.

He retreated, but she pulled him to her. Their lips met again, each seeking and finding the treasure of the other. She had been right. He tasted of wine aged in oak, of fruit and tannin blended in a heady brew and mixed with his own flavor. She sampled the whole palette with her tongue. He did the same to her.

She felt his hands move down her back and slide under her sweater. Breath left her body as he explored the bare flesh before encountering her bra. He paused below her breasts. Her heart beat furiously, and she willed him to go on.

Slowly his thumbs climbed and circled until finally they brushed gently over her nipples. She couldn't breathe at all.

"I want you," he said. "God, how I want you."

"Yes, yes," she urged, wanting him in exactly the same way. "Oh, Sutter, this is more wonderful than I thought possible. I've waited for you."

"*You've* waited," he complained. "I've had to watch you grow up, had to keep my distance while you went through all those damned teenage boyfriends. But now..."

She thrilled at the possessive growl in those last words. Their lovemaking became more intense. She was dying for him to complete it. When his hand roamed under her skirt, seeking the nylon-clad smoothness of her thigh, she throbbed with pleasure.

They slipped downward until they were lying on the sofa, arms and legs all tangled in a glorious entwining of flesh. She became aware of his body on a different level. Feeling the hard length of him against her, every inch of his body pressed to every inch of hers, she knew she was dealing with a man.

His kisses became more demanding, but his hands were gentler. Her clothing was brushed aside. Somehow his shirt was open, their flesh meeting. She sighed and smiled up at him as he partially covered her, one strong thigh nestled between hers. She'd never seen him look so young and carefree and handsome.

"Oh, Sutter," she whispered. "I do love you so."

Her words seemed to click some switch, so abrupt was the change. He pulled away and sat up on the edge of the sofa. He rubbed his face and all emotion disappeared. Then he reached for his shoes as if...as if he intended to leave.

"What are you doing?" she asked.

"What I should have done hours ago. I'm going home."

"But...why?" Self-conscious as he buttoned his shirt and tucked it in, she pulled an afghan over her naked breasts.

His eyes were opaque when he looked at her. The fires of a moment ago were completely doused. "Because I can't give you what you want." He sounded angry. "You want pretty words and flowery speeches. You want marriage and all that. Don't you?"

She couldn't lie to that penetrating gaze. He knew her too well. She nodded, feeling the bridge she had thought existed between them dissolve under her feet.

"Well, I don't. I'll never marry, Meredith. Not you. Not anyone."

His statement shocked her. He'd never said anything like that to her in all the years she'd known him. "But why?"

"Marriage is a fool's game." He flexed his hands together, causing a knuckle to crack in the silence between them. It was the only nervous gesture she'd ever seen him use.

"You wanted me," she accused quietly, not understanding.

"Yes. I'm a man with all the right instincts." He paused, then added, "But I don't...feel that way about you. You're the girl I watched grow up. I...it's difficult to explain."

"I see." She'd thought she had known his heart as well as her own, but she'd been wrong. He'd listened to her ideas about love and marriage, but had shared none of his own.

He paced across the room and turned at the door. "Dammit, Meredith, I never meant to hurt you." He hit the doorjamb with his fist. He looked as desperate as she felt.

His words drove the knife deeper. She felt stunned, unable to think. "I...I know. Thanks, Sutter, for being honest," she finally said. For not taking her love without giving his own; for not hurting her like that.

He stared at her, then opened the door. She pulled the afghan tighter around her and followed in order to lock the dead bolt when he left. She stood by the open door while he put on his coat.

"Will you be all right?" he asked.

It would have been easier if he'd been cruel so she could have hated him. "Yes, of course. Goodbye, Sutter. Be careful. The streets are wet."

He hesitated, then said softly, "Goodbye, Meredith," and left her standing at the door, looking out at the rain....

Meredith pushed away from the door, her thoughts returning to the present. That night had been another time, another place. . . . She wasn't the same woman. A lot of growing could take place in three years.

The episode had established a new focus. Since then she had truly built a life for herself and defined her own identity. She was determined to maintain it. The past three months had stirred the old embers in her, but she knew her feelings were deceptive, the result of tension and worry over her father.

She tossed her purse into a chair, slipped out of her sneakers and, on impulse, struck a match to the logs in the fireplace. She sat on the sofa and tucked her feet under her.

Gazing into the flames, she reviewed the changes she detected in herself. She no longer expected as much from life as she had back then. She'd learned that love given wasn't always returned.

Sorrow pinged through her like the distant sound of a sonar echoing off dreams that had retreated far away. She wondered if Sutter had ever given up any of his dreams.

She glanced at the winter street scene over the fireplace, the one he had thought so desolate. She still liked it, still imagined the lighted windows symbolized families snug in their homes. Of course, the artist's view was from the street. . . .

With her added maturity, she realized she had lately seen herself as the outsider. She longed to be inside, next to the hearth, enclosed within the fire-lit warmth.

When was she going to find someone and fulfill that dream for herself? She was almost twenty-five. Not ancient, but time was slipping away.

She looked at the attractive oak and honey-pine furniture. She'd found and refinished each piece herself so that every table, chair and shelf had personal meaning for her. The walls were painted a warm peach, the woodwork sparkling white. Sunny yellow was splashed about like sudden laughter.

She contemplated the picture again. The time had come for a definitive change in her life. She was tired of winter. She needed the warmth of spring. She needed . . . life.

Chapter Three

Fog draped the central valley in gauzy veils. Meredith watched it swirl and condense on the windowpanes. She stretched, then threw the covers back and headed for the shower. Twenty minutes later, she'd just put the coffee on when the doorbell rang.

She peered through the peephole.

Sutter stood looking out at the foggy landscape, one hand thrust into his back pocket, the other holding a white bag. She opened the door.

He turned. "I come bearing gifts," he said, holding up the bakery sack. His smile was irresistible.

"'Beware of Greeks...'" she muttered thoughtfully.

"I'm of English-Irish extraction." He waved the goodies under her nose, tantalizing her with a whiff of buttery sweetness.

"A white handkerchief would have been enough to indicate surrender. You didn't have to bring breakfast."

He scowled at her. "This is a truce, not surrender."

"Actually, one battle doesn't constitute a full war, does it?"

"Beats me." He lifted and dropped his shoulders. "I don't know what's happening between us these days." His glance held a question as she stepped out of the way.

He came inside, and she closed the door against the impolite, encroaching fog. She led the way into the kitchen. The coffee was done. After pouring two cups, she handed him a plate. He placed his peace offering, four Danish pastries, on it and warmed them in the microwave. They carried the food to the pine table.

"What are you doing out so early?" she asked.

"I thought you might need help getting your stuff to the boat. Your car is pretty small. I brought over a van."

"You rented one?"

He shook his head. "Belongs to the company."

"CNI must be doing well. The boss has a new car, the company owns a van. I'm impressed."

Sutter ate half a pastry in one bite. She had a feeling he'd like to take a chunk out of her hide.

"Like hell," he said.

"I'll exclaim in rapture when I see it. Also the houseboat." Her cool amusement deserted her as she spared a fleeting worry over the boat. "I hope it's habitable. I've packed cleaning supplies."

He glanced around her dining nook and into the kitchen. "You have a knack for making a place a home." He sounded envious.

She was caught off guard. Only the hardness of his face prevented her from saying something foolish, such as volunteering to help him repaint his home and tear out the carpet and put in something bright and cheerful.

The colors had been terrible choices for a residence, gray and burgundy, making his home look like an expensive suite of snooty law offices to her. But then, what did she know? He'd probably picked out the colors. She licked the sweetness from her fingers.

"Your place looked pretty elegant," she said, hiding a grimace of distaste. "I saw the write-up in the Sunday papers back in winter."

He made a grunting sound and finished off the pastry.

"I understand the same decorator did the CNI offices. In the same colors," she added. A tinge of remembered jealousy shot through her.

The decorator's remarks had made it sound as if she and Sutter were *very* close friends. The pictures of the two of them in his town house had confirmed it. They'd been snapped sharing a late-night glass of wine, a fire leaping in the grate, the lights of the city visible through the floor-to-ceiling window along one wall.

Several other photos had disclosed the breakfast room, the study and his bedroom with the concealed electronic panel that controlled everything in the house, right from the bed.

Even though the scenes had been staged, that knowledge hadn't stopped the odd sensation that had ripped through her at the sight of Sutter with another woman in his home.

"Why didn't you come to the open house in January?" he asked, referring to the event the reporter had covered.

The new company headquarters had been open to the press and invited guests. Other guests, she surmised, had been invited to a cocktail party later at his new town house.

His narrow-eyed scowl made her restless. She selected a second pastry before answering. "I wasn't invited."

Before she could raise the Danish to her mouth, a hand closed around her wrist. "I told you the time and date when you were staying with your father over Christmas."

"You mentioned it, yes."

"Well?"

"I don't take anything for granted, Sutter. If you want me at your place, put it in writing."

She knew him so well, she could see the anger steal over him. His lips thinned, his nostrils flared as he exhaled, the frown deepened, forming an inverted V between his eyes. She watched him draw on his control and relax. He released her arm.

"At one time, you'd have been in and out as if you owned the place. You wouldn't let me do a thing without your prior approval at the Sunnyvale condo."

She ate the pastry without tasting it, remembering the time he spoke of. She'd been sixteen when he'd bought his first home.

They'd had a good time fixing it up—arguing and joking while stripping wallpaper, painting, refurbishing the kitchen, putting new tiles in the bathrooms. It had been the one perfect summer of her life. She'd been happy, sure of her future....

"I wouldn't presume so much again," she told him in a quiet tone, meeting his opaque gaze with one of her own.

"Ha," he said, rejecting that statement.

"Besides, I was fixing up my place. You wouldn't believe the hours I spent sanding down this table and chairs."

"I could have used some advice."

"You had a professional decorator this time. You didn't need my suggestions." She smiled and tossed back her hair. "Admit you were relieved not to have to bother with me."

Finally, with a perplexed half smile, he asked, "Why do I get the feeling we're quarreling again?"

"Beats me."

"You're flippant today."

She opened her eyes in mock surprise. "Is that a problem?"

"I don't like it," he murmured as if thinking aloud. "It isn't your usual style."

"What is?"

He didn't answer.

"Tell me the kind of female you like. I won't guarantee to please, but I'll think about it."

He finished his breakfast, wiped his mouth and threw down his napkin as if tossing the gauntlet at her feet.

With a flutter of her lashes, she demanded, "Should I be all flustered and breathless at your overpowering male presence? Is that your kind of woman? Or a sophisticate like your decorator, thin and chic in black knit, with the cool gleam of diamonds or zircon at her throat?"

"Hell," Sutter said, momentarily closing his eyes in frustration. "A man can't talk to you anymore. Why are you so damned prickly?"

She shrugged. "I've got work to do. If you're going to help, come on. We can load your van and be ready to leave when Dad gets here." She picked up her dishes and took them to the kitchen.

He followed with his. She washed, he dried and put away. It was like old times, he thought, yet it wasn't. Things weren't the same. *She* wasn't the same.

"I've got a couple of things I want to stick in my suitcase," she said when they finished. She disappeared down the hall.

He wandered around the small apartment, full of the restless energy that had bothered him for weeks. The restlessness had started when Meredith had come back into his life, he admitted, after that frantic phone call to tell him

Richard was in the hospital. Stopping in the living room, he studied the picture over the mantel.

He didn't like the scene, although the painting itself was good. What had Meredith said? She imagined all the families snug inside, gathered around the fire...something like that.

Stepping closer, he stared at the painted windows. The reflection of firelight gleamed off the panes, but the rooms were empty. No people hurried along the rain-swept street, rushing home to their dinner. Where were the families she saw?

He had the sudden feeling that this painting told him something about Meredith, something basic that he should know. He studied it again. The scene was lonely, he thought, and close in its wake came another revelation... *Meredith* was lonely.

The realization shook him. She'd always had tons of friends. He knew she'd dated an up-and-coming lawmaker during the winter. Her father had mentioned it. Besides, she taught classes at the university. She couldn't be lonely.

Hearing her footsteps, he faced her when she entered the room carrying a soft-sided case and a smaller tote. "I'm ready. Shall we take my stuff to the van?"

"Sure." Obeying her orders, he lugged boxes of groceries and supplies out to the late-model van with CNI emblazoned on the side. An hour later, they were finished. He waited for her to make a decision about her father.

"I suppose I should call and see if he's remembered to leave yet." She went to the phone and dialed.

"Hello," an irritable male voice barked.

"Sir," Meredith said in a game-show-host voice, "answer this question and win a month's cruise on the famous Sacramento delta. Ready? Here's the question: what time were we supposed to get an early start on our vacation?"

"I lost part of a data file," he complained. "It'll be another hour before I can leave."

"Okay. Got a pencil? I'm going to give you directions to the marina." She did so. "Sutter and I—"

"Is he there?"

"Yes. He brought a van over to help—"

"Let me talk to him. He can bring me another copy of the data file. This one was full of errors." His voice trailed off, and she heard the click of the computer keys. He was in his office. As usual.

"Here." She handed the phone to Sutter and went to the kitchen to make sure she'd emptied everything from her refrigerator. She didn't want to come home to green, fuzzy things. All clear. She leaned against the counter and watched the fog swirl.

Ten minutes later, Sutter came to the doorway. "Ready?"

"Yes." She got her purse, and they left.

Traffic was light and the fog thin, so driving was easier on the highway than on the streets. Sutter flicked the radio to a soft-rock station and sang along with a current hit. He had a good voice and was excellent on harmony.

The song lamented lost love and the usual bewilderment of the singer regarding the beloved's motives. Sutter stopped singing and slanted an appraising glance her way.

"What is it?" she asked.

"The men in your life giving you a hard time?" he asked, full of sympathetic amusement.

"Only if I let them." She kept a cool tone to her voice.

"We used to be able to talk," he said softly. "What happened to the girl who shared her dreams?"

Meredith gave him a disbelieving glance. "If you don't know the answer to that, you're dumber than I thought."

"I suppose you're referring to our great night of passion. Are you going to let one moment of insanity spoil a beautiful friendship?"

Trust Sutter to be blunt. "It was more like an hour. And yes, it spoiled our friendship. A woman doesn't like to be reminded of the time she made a complete fool of herself."

"Nor a man."

"When did the great tycoon embarrass himself?"

"When he lost his head in the arms of his best friend." He sighed. "And lost his best friend in the bargain. I miss her."

Meredith felt a wrench in the vicinity of her heart. She was momentarily sorry for him, but that didn't change the facts. Did he think she could go back to being that hero-worshiping young girl who'd thought the sun rose and set with his coming and going, who'd naively believed they were meant for each other? Obviously he did.

But she couldn't. She was a woman now. She needed warmth, companionship, all the promises of life. She needed to be loved.

"Men are so dense," she muttered.

His mouth compressed, his nostrils flared. Portrait of Sutter in anger.

"You women say we don't understand, but do you ever bother to explain? No. You just insinuate men don't come up to scratch without telling us where the hell you itch."

The tension in the van increased to a potential 10.0 on the Richter scale. Meredith broke the taut silence.

"Thank you for that observation. Your acuity regarding women is refreshing." She pointed to the road. "Here's our exit."

* * *

The strange conversation lapsed as she directed him to the boat dock. The fog was really thick on the delta, the numbers on the slips difficult to see. Meredith went to the marina office to check on the location of the houseboat while Sutter waited in the van before parking.

"Lawton, right?" the manager, a rather nice-looking man in his mid-twenties asked when she asked for directions to the berth.

"Yes, Meredith Lawton. I'll be using a houseboat donated to the state—"

"Lucky you," he said, grinning and giving her a quick once-over with light gray-blue eyes. She saw appreciation in his gaze.

"Which one is it?" she asked him.

"Last berth at the end of the floating dock. You'll have some privacy. The couple who lease the next berth have taken their cabin cruiser down to L.A. for the summer. You know how to handle a power boat?"

"Yes."

"You won't have any trouble then. There're instructions on the houseboat for leaving and approaching the dock."

"Good," she said, returning his megawatt smile, but turning down the power a bit. She had enough trouble with the males she knew. She didn't want to encourage another into thinking she was available for a summer romance. "Thanks..."

"Terry Watkins," he supplied. "Here's the key to your place."

She returned to the van, told Sutter to park and stepped off the decking at the marina onto the floating quay. Like a boat, it moved with the currents in the water.

At the far end of the dock, tied to a pier set apart from the rental boats, she found the berth. Her eyes opened wide as she stared at the houseboat that appeared like a specter in the mist, gleaming with polished brass and fresh paint.

"Forty-eight feet if she's an inch," Sutter said, right behind her, his voice strangely quiet in the swirling fog.

The vessel was white with green trim, at least fifteen feet wide. The aft deck was enclosed in a cabana of blue-striped awning with an inner screen of mosquito netting.

Meredith stepped off the floating dock onto the fore-deck. She unlocked the cabin door and went inside, her eyes widening as she looked around. "Good grief," she said.

"Yeah," Sutter said.

The cabin was carpeted in a flecked black-and-green Berber rug. Green curtains shut out the fog. Sofas were built into each side wall with storage drawers underneath. The bridge contained a wooden spoked wheel to guide the craft and a high stool with a padded back for comfort and clear vision.

The kitchen had a microwave, blender, coffeemaker, refrigerator, ice maker, bar—all the accoutrements of modern living, all elegantly fitted into teak cabinets. The wine rack could hold a dozen bottles. Wine glasses hung upside down beneath a cabinet.

"Well, nothing like roughing it," Sutter commented, placing a box of groceries on the countertop. He opened a cabinet and viewed the rose-patterned dishes neatly stacked inside.

"Right." Meredith smiled, euphoric that her worst fears hadn't materialized. She opened and closed doors. "Bed-room with two bunks," she called out. "Bath. Hey, come look at this."

"The table lets down, and the sofas can be used for beds," Sutter informed her, walking down the narrow hall between the bedroom and bath. He stopped in the doorway of the stateroom.

He looked from Meredith to the bed, which was a regular size, large enough to hold a man and a woman comfortably. He fought the images that formed in his mind, but it was no use. Since the night Meredith had called him from the hospital, since he'd held her while she slept in his arms, he'd not been able to forget what it was like to have her slender softness pressed to him.

Their brief discussion on the way to the houseboat only served to bring that night of passion back to his mind more clearly. As if every kiss, every touch, wasn't etched by the acid of desire in his brain. Damn. Why did life have to be so frustrating?

With any other woman, he could take what she offered and not look back. But this was Meredith. She offered her whole self, not just her body, and, God help him, he wanted to take it all!

Aware that this was a bedroom and they were alone, Meredith moved from one luxurious appointment to another. "Look, the dressing table has makeup lights." She flicked them on, then off. She lifted a hinged cover. "A hidden sink. Neat. I'll give Dad the captain's suite and take the bunk room."

Sutter murmured approval of her plan.

She sat on the double bed and bounced up and down. "Firm mattress. Good."

She glanced up. Sutter was leaning against the door frame, staring at her with an intensity of feeling that startled her. She couldn't read the expression in his eyes, but she sensed turmoil within him. His eyes roamed her throat, her chest, down her waist and thighs before returning to her face.

Heat gathered in a heavy knot low in her abdomen. A madly throbbing pulse made itself known at the base of her throat. She lifted a hand to still it.

He turned abruptly and disappeared, slamming the door behind him. She stood and pulled down the sleeves of her sweatshirt, aware of the chill in the air. It was time to quit acting like a tour director and get to work.

When she returned to the fore deck, she met Sutter coming from the van with another box. "Why don't you put things away while I bring them in?" he suggested.

"Okay."

He finished his task first and went to inspect the engine room through a removable panel in the cabana deck. With no cleaning duties to perform, she had the food stored, her clothing unpacked and the beds made in less than two hours. It was noon and there was still no sign of her father.

She climbed a ladder to the roof over the living quarters and found a sun deck with raised lockers along the sides and a safety railing around the edges. Long lounge cushions as well as deck chairs were stored in the lockers.

"All the comforts of home," she murmured.

"And then some." Sutter came up after her.

She surveyed the view from this vantage point. The marsh spread in all directions, the great flat plain of the delta built by the slow erosion of mighty mountains, its towns and roads built by the people who'd chased their dreams across a continent.

The sun had broken through the fog, which was disappearing, and the day had warmed up. Meredith peeled off her sweatshirt. Sutter did the same.

Like her, he wore a T-shirt underneath. Smooth muscles rippled along his arms as he flexed his hands together. He looked like a man ready to hoist anchor and head for distant lands, places as hard and strong and challenging as he was. Her pulses strummed wildly again.

"You look at home on a boat," she said to his back. "Are you thinking of a world cruise?"

He turned and propped his foot on the port locker. "You were always a perceptive little thing," he commented, his eyes hooded so that his feelings were undetectable.

"I'll let you crew for me," she offered grandly.

"When I go, I'll go alone."

The words were spoken gently enough, but they cut all the same. "Of course. Well, *kemo sabe,* I'm hungry. Would you like a ham and cheese sandwich?"

"Yeah."

They went down to the kitchen. She realized she'd reverted to her usual manner with him—a sort of sardonic friendliness that put him at ease. He began whistling while he peered into cabinets. He found chips and put them in a bowl, then he spread mayonnaise on the bread slices she set out.

When their plates were on the table, he told her to wait for him and went to the van. He returned with a bottle of champagne. He opened it and poured a glass for each of them, then took his place at the table. Their eyes met.

"Here's to your voyage."

She clinked her glass to his and took a drink. The bubbles burned her tongue, but the pale liquid went down smoothly.

When they finished eating, Sutter reached over and ruffled her bangs. "Just like old times, huh, kid?"

"Yeah," she agreed, lifting the glass. "Here's to you." She drained the last of the champagne, closing her eyes against his sharp perusal. She didn't want him to detect the way she felt.

And how was that?

Hungry, came the surprising answer. She'd eaten her food and drunk the wine, but she wanted more. A sandwich and a casual friendship were no longer enough to satisfy her, body and soul. She wanted to taste the rapture.

"Why the heavy sigh?" he asked. He yawned and stretched, then tossed his T-shirt aside. His chest rippled with muscle.

She averted her eyes and went out to the aft deck to roll and tie up the striped awning sides so the breeze could blow through. The temperature had soared into the middle eighties, the fog having burned off completely now. Sutter followed and helped.

"My dear father," she answered, gazing toward the road. "I was wondering if he's started yet." She lay on a lounge chair in the shade. Her eyes felt heavy.

Sutter arched one dark brow. "You don't sound concerned."

She laughed. "He'll get here when he gets here."

"Do you want to call? I brought the phone in earlier."

She shook her head, too sleepy to open her eyes. "I'll give him another hour."

Sutter removed a lounger from a locker and set it next to hers. He stretched out on it. Without looking, she was aware of his bare chest within inches of her hand. All she had to do was reach over and caress him. The temptation was irresistible.

His skin was slightly moist, the curly chest hair causing an interesting sensation against her palm. "Why are men so warm?"

"Hot blood," was his unexpected reply. He stopped her exploration by laying his hand over hers. "Watch that you don't get burned."

Sutter could hardly hear his own voice. The blood roared through his ears. He went into immediate and full arousal.

"Your warning's too late." Her laugh was rueful. *Much, much too late.*

"Sleep it off," he advised, putting her hand back on her chair. He should do the same, except right now, he was far from sleep. He fought the need, then laid his hand in the middle of her torso, right below her breasts. "You're warm, too."

Meredith's breath strangled in her throat. She didn't move. Opening her eyes, she encountered something in his gaze she couldn't quite decipher, perhaps a hunger that matched her own. Or dreams that had never found their rapture, either.

"Warm body, cold heart," she said and turned over, unable to face him and the flames in his eyes.

He chuckled finally, a skeptical snort of sound. It was the last thing she heard before she fell asleep.

Something was massaging her abdomen. The purr clued her in just before she opened her eyes. The cat sat down and gazed into her face in an alert, questioning cat fashion.

"Hi," Meredith said, and scratched the creature's ears. It wore no collar or identification, but wasn't skinny and ill-kempt like most strays she'd seen.

The cat purred loudly and stretched out, using his front paws to knead the underside of her breasts.

"I say," she scolded, slipping her hand between the cat and herself, "that's much too intimate for a first meeting. I don't even know your name."

"You shouldn't let him on you," Sutter broke in. "You don't know where he's been hanging out."

She rubbed the cat's head and traced the delicate white blaze down its nose. The rest of its fur was black except for one white sock on a front paw. "He's healthy. Look at how clean and sleek he is."

"You can't always tell by appearances," Sutter warned.

She rolled her head to look at him. He'd raised himself to an elbow and was frowning at her and the cat.

"A person who never takes the risk never knows the bliss," she informed him airily.

The cat scooted up and laid his head on his paws between her breasts. He scrutinized her with his beautiful gray-green eyes.

"Ah, what a charmer you are," she crooned, rubbing down his shiny black coat.

Sutter swung his legs off the lounger and sat upright. The sight of the cat nestled in the warm space between her breasts caused him to react again. It angered him. What the hell was wrong with him? He couldn't control himself around her anymore.

He tried to warn her. "Sometimes the risk is greater than the reward, especially a fleeting reward like passion."

"Before this morning, we'd never discussed that night," she mused, guessing at once what was on his mind. "Why is that?"

"It's best forgotten."

"I'm all grown up, Sutter. Don't treat me like the youngster I was when we met. You weren't so old then, yourself."

He leaped upon her statement. "We grew up together," he agreed. "Like brother and—"

"No," she said sharply. "I had no siblings. You were my friend, my confidant. I'll be your friend if you'll let me, but I won't be your sister."

She rose and placed the tomcat on the lounge chair.

"You seem to be going through some kind of crisis of late." He folded his chair and put it away. After shooing the reluctant cat off, he did the same to hers.

She turned from him and crossed to the leeward side of the boat. He followed.

"What's wrong, Meredith?" he asked, putting aside his problems in real concern for her. He'd been her confidant for years. It was a role he found comfortable.

"Maybe it was my father's heart attack. Maybe it's the fact that I'll be twenty-five in a few days. Maybe I'm tired of waiting for Prince Charming." Meredith bowed to a pretend partner and danced around in a slow waltz, the old sweet yearning rising in her like sap after a bleak winter. She wondered if there really was an ideal man for her. She glanced at Sutter.

He looked her over in a slow, appreciative fashion. "You don't have to worry about being an old maid. There must be any number of potential movers and shakers in Sacramento wanting to know you better."

"A few," she agreed. She gave him the same appraisal he'd bestowed on her. "Perhaps you've spoiled me for other men."

His eyes went dark, the amusement left his face. "Don't."

"What scared you most about the passion between us?" she asked, rushing in where only fools and angels dared go, knowing which category she fitted.

"Getting trapped into marriage."

"I don't remember asking you."

"Touché," he murmured. Then, "You're the daughter of a man I respect more than any other I've ever known."

She simply looked at him, insulted.

"No," he retracted, "that isn't it. It's you."

She made a sound of exasperation. "You say that, but you never clarify it. And you claim *women* are hard to read."

He came to her and took her chin between his thumb and finger, lifting her face. His thighs crowded hers against the rails.

"I've tried to be honest with you," he said, an angry male who didn't like delving into the emotion of a situation. "Sex ruins a friendship, and I value yours. Don't you understand that?"

"Why can't we have both?"

"We just can't."

"Ah, the exclusive *or* of logic circuits," she mocked. "We can have one or the other, but not both."

"Right." He moved away and stared out at the delta, closing himself off.

She mulled over their conversation. Curiosity overtook her. "What's wrong with marriage? My parents didn't think it was an awful trap. Why do you?"

"It brings out the worst in people."

"Not if it's based on love. Love is a force that can change a person's life for the better."

"Love . . . or lust?" he asked softly, dangerously. With a narrowed gaze, he moved in for the kill.

She tried to slide away from his incredible warmth before it melted her insides, but he leaned forward and put his hands on either side of her, trapping her there, her thighs tight against his.

Standing didn't help. He only straightened with her until they were touching along their entire length, chests, stomachs and thighs. The state of his arousal was no secret.

"Well?" he demanded, a snarl of harsh laughter in the word. "You asked for it. Now what are you going to do about it?"

"Jump overboard?" she offered, outwardly cool.

"We'd set the river on fire." He spoke in a low growl.

"It's that polluted?"

"Don't change the subject," he murmured close to her ear, so close he fanned the flames of her irrepressible desire into an inferno. "Let's have this out, once and for all."

"What?" she asked with a wickedly sarcastic smile. "After all, what's in a kiss?" She pressed her hands between them separating the fierce heat of his chest from her breasts.

He laid his hands on her, touching her as she was touching him. She glanced wildly around to see if anyone was looking. No one was in sight at the moment.

"Scared someone will see?" he taunted.

"I don't make love in public."

He slipped his hands around her back, forcing her close again. "Where do you make love?" He looked at her lips, then his glance strayed down to her throat. "How do your lovers make love to you?"

"The usual way."

He bent his dark head and planted a row of stinging kisses along her throat to the throbbing base of her neck. "Like that?"

The attempt to hold him off and to keep her emotions in check wasn't working. A tendril of fear leaped along her nerves. She may have bitten off more than she could chew, as the saying went; a challenge to Sutter wouldn't go unanswered.

"What's gotten into *you* today?" she demanded.

"I've tried to get close to you since your dad was in the hospital. You act like I'm on your most-wanted-dead list half the time; at others, like today, you give me the come-on as if you want me for a lover. Which is it?"

"Both."

He shook his head, the dark waves reflecting the sun in a gleaming array of light. "You can't have it both ways. Make up your mind. I'll be your lover or your friend, but not both."

"You put *lover* in the same context as *enemy.*"

"Maybe they are the same." He shifted against her.

She couldn't believe the swell of desire his movement caused. She burned with it. An ache started inside as she felt his body throb with the unmistakable hunger of male passion.

"Maybe. But enemy or lover, I'm still not scared of you," she asserted, defiant and foolish to the bitter end.

"Bravely spoken. I wonder if it's true," he mocked.

"Try me."

"I'm tempted."

Her nerves stretched to the breaking point. He was in a strange mood. He'd never challenged her in quite this way. But then, she'd never challenged him exactly like this, either. Maybe both of them were due for a change.

She twisted out of his grasp, and he let her go. She hoped he didn't notice the trembling of her legs as she walked forward. With Sutter, it wasn't wise to show weakness. She spotted her car coming down the road. "There's my car. Finally."

"Just in time. A storm was brewing."

She whipped around, her hair striking her cheek as the breeze caught it. "Don't offer choices you're not prepared to honor," she advised. "I'll choose the lover over the friend any day, and let you worry about the risks."

With that, she strode forward to welcome her tardy parent aboard.

Chapter Four

Meredith paddled about on the float, a giant rubber tube, the flippers on her feet making her progress across the mouth of the slough easy and rapid.

Stopping, she dropped the sampling nozzle into the water, watched for the three-foot mark on the cord, then flicked the lever to open the spring-loaded door. After pulling the sample up, she released the few ounces of water into a bottle and recorded temperature, location and depth on the label. Proceeding in an orderly manner across the inlet, she finished the task.

For her return to the houseboat, which was moored across the river channel at a marina, she leaned against the tube and paddled leisurely, occasionally looking over her shoulder to line up with the boat. She sang an old song about cruising down the river and gazed at the sunset.

Suddenly another voice joined in, a male voice that blended in perfect harmony with hers, making her sound much better than she actually was. She pivoted the tube so she faced forward.

Sutter stood on the deck next to the swim-out, waiting to help her aboard. He wore old cutoffs and nothing else. A flutter of nervousness ran over her and her breath went raspy. He disturbed her, mentally and physically. She didn't like it.

It's just Sutter, she reminded herself sharply.

When she reached the stern, she handed the wire basket of vials to him. While he put them away, she removed her fins and tossed them over the transom. Taking a deep breath and holding it, she threw herself backwards, flipping upside down and kicking out of the harness that held her in.

She surfaced just as Sutter reached for the tube. He hauled it onto the deck, then held out a hand to her when she stood up on the broad step at water level that made it easy for swimmers to climb aboard. She shook her head and clambered over the transom step to the deck.

His strong clasp steadied her as the houseboat rolled with a swell from a passing power craft. She briefly leaned against his chest, then righted herself.

"Thanks." She crossed to a chair and grabbed her towel.

"You've put in a long day," Sutter mentioned, glancing at the disappearing sun.

"I wanted to finish this side of the river and the mouth of the slough before heading upriver tomorrow." She wrapped the towel around her hair and twisted it to squeeze out the water.

"How would you like to join me and your dad for dinner tonight? There's a great restaurant at the marina."

She shook her hair back and ran her fingers through it to comb out the tangles. "I'm too tired to go out. I don't want to dress. You and Dad can go."

"Richard said you were working hard."

"There's a lot of ground, uh, water, to cover." She managed a grin, although the effort was almost too much for her. She might have overdone it today, she thought.

"Tell you what, I'll bring dinner over to you later, after I talk to Richard about a project we're thinking of bidding on."

"No, thanks."

Avoiding his hard perusal, she went in and headed for the shower. Fifteen minutes later, she turned the dryer on her hair and blew out the excess moisture. After a minute of serious concentration, she donned lacy briefs and a nightshirt that came to her ankles. Made of heavy cotton knit, it was modest enough to be seen in. She went into the main cabin.

As she'd expected, Sutter and her father were gone. They were probably still waiting for a table. On Friday night the restaurants in the marinas swarmed with boat people and town people, who showed up for the fresh seafood served there.

The river had been peaceful all week. She and her father had worked together on their various projects, absorbed as always in the task at hand. Sutter had called several times and talked to her father. She'd known he was meeting them tonight at the new marina farther down the river.

She drifted out to the aft deck, where netting kept out the mosquitoes, and settled into a lounge chair, too tired to think about food. She'd eat in a minute. Right now, it was better to rest. She'd been working like a demon all week.

Without warning, a warm weight settled in the middle of her body. The tomcat gave his face a wash, then nestled with his head on his paws between her breasts, his favorite position. She felt his soft purr of satisfaction when she stroked his broad back and wished her life was as uncomplicated.

He'd adopted her and her father and had tagged along on the trip down the delta, living on the boat with them. She'd worried about him getting lost, but Terry, back at their home marina, had assured her the cat was a survivor.

"Hey, T.C., where you been today?" she crooned. T.C. was short for tomcat, not very original but correct as to gender, Terry had assured her. Soothed by the cat's husky purr, she let the tension drain out of her.

Closing her eyes, she listened to the music drifting over the deepening twilight from the restaurant. At least it was peaceful music. The melody of "Stardust" added just the right melancholy note to the evening.

Footsteps along the quay woke her from a doze a few minutes later. Sutter stepped onto the deck, a large box in his hand. The familiar quiver rushed through her, disrupting her calm.

"Dinner, madam," he intoned in a deep voice.

The cat slipped away into the dark.

"What was that?" Sutter asked.

"The cat."

"The stray? You brought him along?"

She laughed. "It was more like he took charge. Like someone else I could name. Where's Dad?" Her nerves fluttered again, and she wondered if she wanted her father there for protection—from Sutter or for him?

"He's arguing about the locations of the best fishing holes with some guy he met earlier this week up at the bar."

She followed Sutter into the air-conditioned cabin, where he deftly spooned her meal onto a plate and joined her at the table with a glass of wine for each of them.

"I could take to this kind of life," she murmured, realizing she was hungry and that it was nice to be served.

Sutter had changed from the cutoffs to tan linen slacks and a blue silk shirt. The open throat allowed a glimpse of black curly chest hair. He was devastatingly male, and every sense of caution she'd ever known kept trying to flee.

"You like being on the river?" he asked, raising the glass to his lips. He took a drink and swallowed. He, too, looked as if he'd been working hard all week.

"It's okay," she conceded.

She picked up her fork and took a bite of crab primavera. The seasoning was perfect, and she realized she was famished. He waited in stark silence while she polished off the last bites of the meal.

"That was wonderful. Thank you," she said. She picked up the wineglass and sipped, feeling contentment wash over her again.

Glancing at him from beneath her lashes, she saw him gazing out at the river, his expression harsh, the inverted V between his eyes once again. He didn't look angry so much as worried.

"What's wrong?" she asked, setting the glass down.

"What? Oh, nothing." His mind was definitely elsewhere.

"Why the heavy gloom?"

He focused his attention on her. "It's a problem at work."

His gaze roamed over her face and down her throat. Her breasts immediately tensed, the nipples hardening to points against the cotton knit. He stared at the provocative peaks, seemingly fascinated. She crossed her arms over her chest, hiding the evidence of her reaction to him.

"Technical?" she asked to divert him.

"Personal."

"Oh."

He shoved a lock of black hair off his forehead. "Not that kind of personal. My secretary has a problem. Some guy she knew in Sunnyvale found out where she moved and is hanging around."

"How do you mean, hanging around?"

Sutter grimaced in irritation. "He keeps showing up wherever she goes—on the street outside her house, outside the office when she leaves to go home, at the grocery store."

"That would make me nervous."

"It's driving her crazy. Me, too."

"Is he watching you, too?" Meredith asked in surprise.

"No, but Linda is upset. She mixed up two appointments this week and mailed a letter for one company to its rival. It caused some problems with my suppliers."

Meredith clucked sympathetically.

"I don't know what to do about him. My security chief talked to the police. They said they couldn't arrest a person for being on a public street."

Meredith took her plate to the sink, washed it and put it away. She removed frozen yogurt from the freezer and prepared two dishes with fresh strawberries for topping. She served Sutter, then resumed her seat.

"Remember the psychologist I told you about?" she asked.

"The one you've selected for your father?"

She nodded. "Genna will be visiting with us for a few days starting Sunday. You could ask her advice on how to get rid of somebody like that."

Sutter's noncommittal grunt sounded doubtful.

"She could probably give you a personality profile."

He considered the suggestion. "Maybe that would help. Give me her number and I'll call her from the office tomorrow."

Meredith wrote it down and gave the paper to him. He stuck it in his pocket. They ate the yogurt and strawberries, then returned to the aft deck with their wine.

From the other end of the marina, the music and murmuring conversation from couples eating on the covered veranda added a muted backdrop to the quiet river noises. At one of the tables, she saw her father bent over a map with his fishing friends.

"Richard seems to be enjoying himself," Sutter commented, his mind following her train of thought. "He looks more relaxed than I've ever seen him."

Meredith laid her hand on Sutter's arm for a brief instance. "He told me this morning he didn't realize retirement would be so much fun. I think it's going to work out."

"Is he spending too much time on my projects? I've tried not to push him, or overload him."

"No. He fishes in the early morning, goes over your stuff, has lunch, naps, exercises, then goes fishing again. He loves studying the design problems you've sent him." She laughed. "He even makes me help him draw up the timing diagrams to make sure all those little gates are open when they're supposed to be."

"Maybe I'd better put you on the payroll," Sutter suggested.

"No, thanks, I'll stick to my own thing."

"You can't take anything from me anymore, can you?"

The pleasant ambiance disappeared like a firefly's light. "I don't need anything from you," she answered softly.

"Right," he said. "Thanks for the number of the shrink. Maybe I'll call her."

He stood, but instead of storming off as she expected, he propped a foot on the gunwale and quaffed the remainder of his wine. She could sense his anger and wondered why he was so easily infuriated by her these days.

"I've got to go," he said, but for another minute he made no move to do so. He lingered, looking down at her. Then he was gone. The tension remained long afterward.

She stayed on the aft deck for another hour. Her father returned and joined her.

"Sutter gone?"

"Yes."

"Did you enjoy your dinner?"

"It was very good."

They were silent, listening to the lap of water against the side of the boat.

"Something wrong between you and Sutter?"

"Wrong?" she repeated cautiously. She didn't know how much her father had intuited about them.

He stretched his long legs out and crossed them at the ankles, picture of a man at ease. "I was nervous about your dating when you were younger," he said after a few seconds, "but your mother told me we'd done our part. Either you had the sense to make good decisions or you didn't. When she died . . ."

His voice trailed off into the hush of darkness. She waited, sensing his memories of those days of grief.

"I wasn't there for you when you needed me the most," he continued softly, "but thank God Sutter was."

"You were lost in your own pain," she reminded him, reaching out to squeeze his arm.

"Yes. To lose your mother was to lose my soul." He fell silent, then, when he spoke, the words came hesitantly, as if they were hard to say. "She was the love of my life. I'd hoped you'd find someone like that."

Meredith's throat closed for a minute. "Me, too."

"You and Sutter used to be friends." He paused again, giving her a chance to comment, but she remained silent. "If you want to talk to me...about anything...I'll listen," he finished. "I want you to know I'm here for you. If you need me."

"Thanks." She jumped up. "I think I'll go on to bed. It's been a long day."

"And you fuss at me about working too hard," he chided, following her inside the cabin.

She laughed. "I have about ten thousand samples to take, and the time keeps ticking away."

Once in bed, although her body was tired, her mind wouldn't shut off. Genna was due to arrive on Sunday. She so wanted her father to like her friend.

A thud and a purr told her T.C. had arrived. He settled against the pillow next to her head. She patted him. "At least you don't have any hang-ups about sleeping with me."

"Hello in there," a voice called.

Meredith peered out the window, put down the paring knife and rushed to the foredeck.

Genna's silver curls blew around her oval face as she stepped aboard. She wore shorts and a bright print top tied at her waist. Two years younger than Dr. Lawton, the psychologist had been a widow for five years and was Meredith's prime candidate for the position of wife and stepmother.

"Welcome aboard," Meredith exclaimed.

The women hugged, and Meredith took the light piece of luggage to carry inside.

"Come on in. I'm so glad you're here. Dad's at the store. He'll be back in a moment, then we'll have lunch."

"This is marvelous," Genna said. Her blue eyes skimmed from one luxurious item to another. "Air-conditioning, too. I can't believe it."

"You'll share the bunk room with me. It's through here. I've got the upper berth. You can have the lower."

Genna laughed in approval when she saw the snug space and the tiny ladder to the top bunk, reminding Meredith why she enjoyed the older woman. Genna had an enthusiastic attitude toward life and obviously relished new experiences.

Oh, her father was just going to *love* Genna!

Meredith peered impatiently toward the marina store. They'd moved back to their original berth yesterday so she could exchange her filled containers for empty ones. She was making good progress on her sampling. Her father was thoroughly involved with Sutter's designs and trying to best his friends at fishing. Things were going well.

"Here he comes," Meredith told Genna.

He looked good for a man of sixty-five. Tall, two inches more than Sutter, with distinguished wings of gray in his dark mahogany hair, he walked with the energy and confidence of a younger man. He was dressed in tan shorts, deck shoes and a jauntily striped polo top of blue, yellow and white.

"I'd know you were father and daughter," Genna murmured. "The same slender, long-boned body, the same hair. Are his eyes hazel like yours?"

"Yes. Mine have more green, though. My mother had dark green eyes with brown flecks, although her hair was blond."

"Hmm," Genna said.

Meredith refrained from asking for Genna's first impressions, even though she was dying to know. This matchmaking was hard on the nerves. She wanted them to like each other... heck, she wanted them to fall in love at first sight!

"Here's the lettuce." He swung onto the deck and came into the roomy cabin. "Hello," he said, catching sight of Genna.

"Dad, this is Dr. Genna Carlisle. Genna, Dr. Richard Lawton. Now you two Ph.D.s can go sit in the shade, and I'll serve lunch out there in... um... ten minutes."

"Hello, Richard," Genna said, extending a neatly manicured hand with pale pink polish on the nails. Her outfit was a deep rose pink. Meredith realized Genna's color was rosy, too. So the poised doctor was a little excited, hmm?

"Genna, glad to meet you. Meredith has told me about your flower-arranging class. I'm thinking of taking it up if the fish don't start biting soon. Do you fish?"

"My husband and I went to Montana for trout every year."

"All right!" Richard said. "We'll show those two—"

"Out," Meredith ordered. "Here're your drinks." She handed them each a tall frosted glass of iced tea laced with some exotic herb blends she'd found at the store.

Smiling with relief—at least they hadn't taken an instant dislike to each other—she spooned up pasta salad, arranged grilled chicken over it and added cold slices of melon to the plates. From the oven, she removed a hot, crusty loaf of San Francisco sourdough bread, wrapped it in a napkin and placed it in a basket.

She loaded a tray and carried the meal to the table set up on the deck. Genna and her father, she was pleased to note, were chattering like old friends.

"Lunch," she announced, propping the tray on the edge of the table and unloading it. She returned to the kitchen for her drink and brought the pitcher out for refills.

"Meredith, what was the name of the town in Montana where the chef looked like a hoodlum and cooked like Julia Child?" Richard wanted to know.

"Red Bluff or something like that—"

"Red Lodge," he remembered. He went on with his story, sending the two women into gales of laughter as he related his worries about a thug cooking their expensive French dinner.

"Mother and I ate our food without a qualm," Meredith joined in. "Dad wanted to bring in a dog to sniff everything first."

"I think women have stronger constitutions than men," he retorted, defending his caution.

"I'm glad there's one male in the world who recognizes the female as the stronger sex," Genna said.

"Oh, no, not another one of those independent women," Richard groaned. A shiny red vehicle entered the marina parking lot and stopped by Meredith's compact car. Richard brightened. "Look, it's Sutter."

Sutter came down the floating dock and dropped lightly to the deck. There was a pause while he looked at Genna. "Dr. Carlisle, I presume," he murmured, tongue-in-cheek.

"Do you two know each other?" Richard asked, surprised.

"On your daughter's advice, I telephoned Dr. Carlisle about a business matter yesterday. She's our newest consultant." He smiled at Genna and Richard, then flicked a glance at Meredith, who sat there like a stick, unable to summon a smile.

"Have you had lunch?" Richard asked, then, without waiting for an answer, he turned to Meredith. "Do we have enough for one more?"

"Sure." She rose and hurried inside, an acute sense of dissatisfaction plaguing her. Once she reached the kitchen, she stood there a minute, frowning into space.

She hadn't expected to see Sutter again so soon and hadn't been prepared to face him after their strange argument about friends and lovers. Besides, she was already tense over Genna and her father's attitudes toward each other. Please, one thing at a time, she silently prayed.

After a minute, her heart stopped chugging like a train on a long climb and settled down. She grabbed a plate from the shelf and tossed ice into a glass. She was laying a fork on the plate just as Sutter came in.

She noted the deep V etched between his brows. He looked as if he hadn't slept well. The problems at the office were really getting to him.

"Okay if I wash up first?" he asked.

"Sure."

He stared at her for another five seconds, as if expecting a further statement from her. She raised her brows, silently asking if there was something more he wanted.

With a sound that might have been a snort of exasperation or a sigh of resignation, he walked on down the passageway.

Meredith carried his plate and glass out to the table and resumed her seat. She, Genna and her father waited until Sutter joined them before beginning the meal.

"This is good," he complimented Meredith. "I had breakfast about the time the sun came up, and that was hours ago."

"Thank you," she murmured.

"You must have gone to the office," Genna commented, after it was obvious Meredith had nothing else to say.

He glanced at his clothing. "The country club. I had a meeting with some venture capitalists this morning. It's hard to get a loan these days unless it's backed by Fort Knox."

Richard shook his head. "I don't know how you deal with all that business stuff. I hated filling out reports."

"So do I," Sutter admitted. He spoke to Genna. "I had my security chief speak to Fisher. He told him we were going to get a restraining order if he kept it up. It seems to have helped. Linda didn't see him yesterday afternoon or this morning."

"Sometimes letting them know you're not going to put up with harassment takes care of the problem. Sometimes it doesn't." This last was spoken in a cautious tone.

"What's happening?" Richard asked.

"My secretary's being hassled by a young man who's taken a fancy to her," Sutter said. "He used to mow her yard when she rented that cottage in Sunnyvale. Then he started doing other things for her, small repairs and such, without being asked."

"She lives in Sacramento now, doesn't she?" the scientist asked. "Wasn't that Linda on the phone the other day?"

Sutter nodded. "She was relieved to move. Then a month ago, he showed up at her door, offering to paint her new place. She told him that she didn't need anything done and got rid of him, but he hangs around on the street, at the apartment and at work."

"This type of situation is frightening for a woman," Genna said. "She doesn't understand the man's intentions."

"It's too bad she got involved with him," Sutter began.

Meredith took umbrage at that statement. "Hiring someone to mow the lawn is hardly an involvement," she informed him, her eyes flashing at this injustice. "It isn't Linda's fault that the guy is a nut case."

Richard looked worried. "How old is this man?"

"Hardly more than a boy," Sutter answered. "He's in his late teens or early twenties."

"Is he dangerous?"

Genna paused in refilling her glass. "That's impossible to say at this point. We don't know the history of his psychosis."

"We've found his aunt. We're hoping she can tell us," Sutter explained. He turned to Genna. "I'd like for you to interview her tomorrow. I'll pick you up and drive you to her house, if that's convenient for you."

Genna looked at Meredith. "Will that delay your research?"

"I don't think so. Since I've been working on Saturday and sometimes on Sunday, I can take a day off."

Dr. Lawton glanced at Sutter. "We had a similar case at work a few years back that ended in tragedy. Do you remember? The man shot his way past the security gate and killed several people, including the woman, before a police sharpshooter got him."

"That's the extreme form of obsessive behavior," Genna said. "Unfortunately, it's found in two distinct personality types. One shows an early pattern of violence and inability to take no for an answer. Everything must revolve around his wants and needs."

"Fisher doesn't seem violent," Sutter mused. "In fact, he's just the opposite—quiet, timid, almost too polite."

"That can be a shell to hide his real emotions," Genna warned.

"What's the other type?" Meredith asked.

"The man who comes to depend totally on his partner. In these emotionally dependent cases, the man is rarely physically abusive, at least not until the woman tries to leave. Instead, he smothers the object of his desire with attention."

"I knew a guy like that in college. He dated a friend of mine. We thought he was wonderful—flowers, phone calls at all hours—but then . . ."

"Then it became too much," Genna finished for her. "I hope your friend avoided him."

"She did. But it's also a nice fantasy, at least for a while," Meredith added, her manner softening.

"Fantasy?" Sutter turned his soul-searching gaze on her.

"That a man is so obsessed with you, he can't bear to leave you or have you look at another man."

"True," Genna said. "But most people, even romantic young girls, can distinguish between a great *love* and an obsession after a while. The first is true caring for the other person; the second stems from purely selfish needs."

A sudden smile smoothed the worried lines on Sutter's face. "No man would have a chance to feed that kind of obsession with Meredith. She'd cut him to ribbons with her sharp tongue."

"That's true," Richard agreed, grinning at his daughter's indignant expression. "By the way, would you women like to have dinner at the Angler's Inn tonight? I understand they have dancing later in the evening. Sutter and I could give you gals a twirl."

He looked at Genna, his hazel eyes bright with interest. Meredith had to swallow twice to remove the lump from her throat. She darted a glance at Sutter, meeting his eyes for the first time since he'd arrived.

She looked away, her thoughts turned inward on the differences between love and obsession. She examined her own motives. As a teenager, she'd thought Sutter would have to love her if she loved him. That was the way it happened in books and movies. She realized her attitude had been totally selfish, focused on her wants, assuming he wanted the same. Looking back, Meredith realized that he had held back, never revealing his deepest emotions.

After that fiasco in her apartment, she'd tried so hard to build a life for herself, but cast back into Sutter's company since her father's illness, she found her old feelings for him being resurrected. Didn't a person ever outgrow a first love?

Of course they did, she told herself.

The real problem was that she hadn't yet found someone to take his place in her romantic fantasies. As soon as she did, she'd be able to put Sutter in his proper place as merely a friend.

This fascination was probably what Sutter had said it was—merely an unfulfilled sexual attraction that had existed between them for a long time. Once they made love, really made love, it would be over. Even she, romantic that she was, knew affairs didn't last.

She glanced up and realized the other three were looking at her. The thinning of Sutter's lips indicated his growing anger.

"What?" she asked.

"Sutter said he'd go. How about you?" her father asked.

"Dancing?" she hedged. To be in his arms would add fuel to the flames that already consumed her. "I guess so."

"I'm underwhelmed by your delight," Sutter commented.

"I was thinking of something else." She gave him a defiant glance, then caught Genna's eyes on her with the dawning light of understanding in their depths.

"Let me help you with the dishes," the older woman suggested. "We can decide what to wear tonight."

"We could fish this afternoon," Richard suggested while the women cleared the table. "I have some old clothes you can wear."

"I have a change in the car," Sutter said, moving so Meredith could get around him to the door. Their knees brushed, and he looked at her as if he'd felt a jolt of electricity, too. She quickly went inside.

"Do you want to wash or dry?" Genna asked, following her.

"I'll do both. You go back out and relax."

Genna pretended to be shocked. "And leave you in here slaving alone? I'll do no such thing."

Meredith smiled wryly. "I'll dry then."

Genna ran water into the sink and added a squirt of soap. She washed the glasses. "Sutter is an interesting person. Not many executives these days care about their employees' problems. I've known some who refused to help the police in cases like this."

"He's always been a very responsible individual," Meredith told her friend.

"A rare trait in this day of giant conglomerates and profit margins, but one that's characteristic of firstborn children. Was he the oldest in his family?"

Meredith dried and put a glass away. "Um-hmm. He had a half brother. His parents were divorced. I don't know how old he was, but he must have been young when that happened. His brother was only six years younger."

"His mother remarried?"

"Yes, but the brother was from his father's second marriage. His mother married a man with two daughters, both older than Sutter. I don't think he knows them very well. All his family live in the east. His half brother died a few years ago. Sutter was grim after the funeral, but he wouldn't say much about it."

"Does he confide in you?"

"No." Meredith finished the glasses and started on the plates. "You know, I just realized I really know very little about him, only the barest facts of his early life." It was almost as if he had no past before he'd met her and her father.

"He and Richard are fond of each other."

"Yes."

Genna peered out the window at the men, who were fishing off the end of the pier. "Male bonding rituals," she murmured. "Did you ever feel left out?"

Meredith gave her friend an amused glance. "No, Sutter saw that I was included in all their activities. Are you analyzing me and my misspent youth, Genna?"

The older woman laughed. "All right, I confess. I do tend to delve into other people's psyches without an invitation. I'll watch it from now on."

"That's all right. I have a question or two of my own."

"Oh?"

"How do you like my father?"

Genna let out the dishwater and rinsed the sink. "Do I detect a bit of matchmaking here?"

"Yes."

"I think Richard is delightful. So far I like him a lot, but then, anyone who can raise a daughter like you can't be all bad."

Meredith had to grin. "I guess I asked for that. I won't push, either. Let's just all be friends."

Genna agreed and went to the bunk room to freshen up. Meredith watched her father and Sutter as they talked, their faces intent, a deep mutual respect observable in their manner to each other. Sutter had fit so smoothly into her life, she'd never wondered about his own before he'd become part of her family.

Three years ago he'd told her he'd never marry. She'd taken it as a personal reference, that he'd never want to marry her, but he'd said he'd not marry anyone. Why?

It was obvious he'd make a wonderful husband. He was kind, considerate, thoughtful. He had a sense of humor. He was hardworking, smart and sexy enough for a movie idol. What more could a woman want?

More importantly, what did *he* want?

A little mental probing seemed called for. Fools and angels, she thought, but she determined to find out all she could about Sutter Kinnard...and the past that had shaped him.

Chapter Five

"Miner Slough, Prospect Slough, Cache Slough." Genna read the names off the wall map next to their table. "Sounds like the gold country was right here in the heart of the delta."

"It started here," Sutter explained. "The gold washed down out of the mountains in the spring floods. It was found in most of the sloughs."

"Steamboat Slough. The steamboats brought goods from San Francisco to Sacramento, didn't they?"

"And the miners," Richard confirmed. "The forty-niners who could afford it rode the steamboats up the Sacramento. From there, the smart ones followed the trail of gold up the rivers to the mother lode in the Sierras."

"What an exciting time that must have been," Meredith mused.

"Dangerous," Sutter corrected. "Why do you think there's so many Dead Man's bluffs, creeks and fords in the mountains?"

"Life-and-death situations are pretty exciting." She insisted on her version of the past.

Sutter, to her surprise, grinned and shook his head at her naïveté. When he reached out to ruffle her bangs, she dodged his hand. He dropped it back to the arm of his chair.

Music interrupted the conversation as the band swung into a loud rendition of a popular number to start the entertainment. This was obviously the signal people had been waiting for. The dance floor filled immediately.

"Shall we?" Richard asked the older woman.

Laughing, he and Genna joined the couples, mostly in their twenties, in gyrating about the floor. Meredith spared a moment's worry about her father's heart, then relaxed.

"Look, he's standing in one place and letting Genna do most of the work," she pointed out to Sutter. "That rascal."

"Smart man," was Sutter's only comment.

The band segued into a slow number, and the movement on the floor changed to match the new tempo. Her father and Genna laughed and talked, then became silent as the melody caught them up in its gentle cadences.

By now, she and Sutter were practically the only ones still at their table. She couldn't decide if she wanted to dance with him or not. Not that it mattered. He wasn't going to ask.

"Do you remember our ballroom dancing lessons?" He turned his gaze from the dancers to her.

"Of course. You caught on right away."

"It helped me when I launched my own business." At her questioning glance, he continued, "I've had to go to a lot of functions since starting the company, Chamber of Commerce parties and that sort of thing. You were right. A person needs to be accomplished in the social graces as well as the technical fields.''

''Was that the argument I used?''

''Yes. Don't you remember?''

She shook her head.

He watched the dancers for a minute. ''What do you want for your birthday? It's only five days away.''

''Nothing.''

''Nothing from me,'' he elaborated, his mouth grim.

A reckless energy washed over her. ''That's not true. You know what I want from you.''

''For two cents—'' He stopped when she opened her purse and searched out some change.

''Here.'' She slapped two pennies onto the table.

Their eyes met and locked. She refused to look away even when she began to feel dizzy from the force of his anger. The return of the other couple to the table ended the duel. Meredith thought the air between her and Sutter must have been red-hot, but no one seemed to notice.

''Were you named after Sutter of Sutter's Fort?'' Genna asked, studying the map again after taking a cool drink of sangria.

''No, it was my mother's maiden name and goes back several generations in my hometown.''

Genna's attentive interest invited further information, but Sutter didn't add anything. What skeletons did he hide with his silence, Meredith wondered.

''How did you get out here?'' Genna asked.

''Richard offered me a job when I finished school. I took it, liked the area and have been here since.''

''He told me he stayed for the skiing and sailing,'' Meredith put in. ''Personally, I think he likes the work.''

Genna turned to Meredith. "Richard told me you were born in California. I hadn't realized that. The way Americans move from place to place, it's rare to meet a native."

"I've only been out of the state a few times," Meredith confessed, then gave her friend an impish smile. "When one lives in paradise, why look for anything else?"

"Spoken like a true daughter of the Bear Republic," Sutter said. He glanced at his watch. "I need to go. I've an early meeting before the interview with Fisher's aunt."

"Yes. I'm tired, too." Meredith stood, relieved to have the evening come to a close.

"You young folks can go," Richard said. "Genna and I still have some dancing to do."

Meredith was startled at her father's declaration, then she laughed in approval. "Don't let him wear you out," she cautioned.

Sutter volunteered to walk Meredith to the houseboat, and she had no choice but to accept. Fortunately the quay was too narrow for him to walk beside her, although she was aware of him right behind her on the swaying planks. After stepping on board, she turned and said good-night.

"Here's something you forgot." He took her hand and dropped the two pennies into her palm, then closed her fingers over them. "Don't issue a challenge unless you know what the risk is," he advised in sardonic tones.

She dropped the change into the breast pocket of his jacket. "I'm not the one worried about the consequences. You are."

He touched her chin. "With good reason."

"Name one." She wanted to smash the invisible barrier he placed around his inner thoughts.

After ramming both hands into his pockets as if to control them, he stepped onto the deck. He stared at the reflection of the moonlight on the gently lapping water, his mood changing to one of introspection. "You could get pregnant."

The forthright statement caused a ripple of shock to flow from her neck down to her toes. She decided to counter his bald fact with one of her own . . . just to see his reaction. "I like children."

He snorted. "Raising them alone would be tough."

"You're not that callous. Are you?" she demanded, not quite sure.

"Maybe," was all he said, closing the door on his thoughts.

Exasperated, she demanded, "Was your parents' marriage so awful that you can't bear the thought of trying it yourself?"

"Yes."

The simple declaration brought her to a thoughtful pause. Pity touched her heart. "You were so young when they divorced. Surely you don't remember—"

"I remember."

The flat answer left no room for rebuttal. "What about now? Your mother and stepfather have been married for over ten years. Aren't they happy?"

She saw the shrug of his shoulders silhouetted against the marina lights. She sensed a loneliness in him, one that reached far into his past. It was almost as if, after all these years of knowing him, she was just beginning to see inside to the real Sutter Kinnard. Dear God, to feel sorry for him . . . a person would have to be insane to pity anyone as hard as he was.

"They seem to be," he finally said.

"My parents were wonderfully suited to each other," she mused aloud. "I remember the laughter. . . ."

"That's what Richard said one time, that more than anything he missed her laughter. When you have something special, I guess it's pretty hard to let it go."

Meredith heard the strain in Sutter's voice, saw it in the hard lines of his mouth. He sounded almost envious. But that was ridiculous. She doubted he'd ever missed another person the way she and her father had missed her mother.

"I had a friend once," he continued. "But I lost her somehow and I'm not even sure why."

She clenched her fists but said nothing.

He sighed, an admission of defeat. "A few minutes of passion make a poor substitute for years of friendship."

"You didn't want to let her grow up."

"Dammit, Meredith," he muttered, a deep-voiced growl, "just because I didn't make love to you doesn't mean I don't see you as a woman. I know you're an adult. I know you work and plan and worry over the future like everyone else does."

A sob rose to her throat. She wanted to hold him and soothe him and tell him they could go back to the way they used to be.

"I wish I understood you. I don't know what you want from me." He spread his hands in a weary gesture.

"Nothing. People change. Life is different now, that's all." She heard the sadness in her own voice. He did, too.

"Don't." He pulled her to his chest. Resting his cheek against her hair, he spoke so softly she almost couldn't make out the words. "If we made love, I'd have to marry you—"

"I've never made that kind of demand."

"—but you deserve a hell of a lot better than me." His brief laugh was bitter.

She patted his chest and put distance between them. "I've got to go in now. Are you going to give me a good-night kiss?"

He stiffened at her banter, then relaxed and bent his head close to hers. "Is a kiss all you want?"

"We-e-ll," she drawled, "I'll settle for that."

"That's all it'll ever be."

She laughed, then nipped at his lower lip until he captured her mouth and deepened the kiss into a real one. She flirted with him through the kiss, stroking, withdrawing, until he probed her mouth hungrily. With an effort, he broke away.

"You could drive a man crazy." He leaped to the dock and strode to shore. He didn't look back when he reached his car, but got in and drove off.

"Picture of a man on the run," she told T.C. when he jumped into her lap. "Is he running from me or himself?"

Sutter returned at eight the next morning. Meredith had slept late and was still in her nightshirt. Richard was already out with his fishing buddies. Genna had dressed and was ready to go. The interview with Fisher's aunt was at ten.

"Here, read this," he said, coming into the main cabin and handing the psychologist a note.

Meredith had never seen him so grim. Anger expressed itself in every line of his body, was etched in the frown on his face. She poured a cup of coffee, tossed in two ice cubes to cool it to drinking temperature and handed the cup to him.

"Thanks." He flicked her an opaque glance before taking a large swallow.

"What is it?" she asked. "Trouble?"

"With a capital *T.*" He didn't elaborate.

Genna handed the note to Meredith, who scanned it quickly. In crude block letters, it warned Linda to quit seeing other men or she would be punished.

"How do you think he'd punish her?" Meredith asked, returning the note to Sutter. A chill, as if evil had invaded the luxurious houseboat, assailed her. She sat at the table and warmed her hands by wrapping them around her coffee cup.

"I assume he'll try to kill her. That's what my security chief has decided."

"We'll have to check his past at once," Genna concluded. "If he has a history of violence..." A worried frown nicked two lines between her eyes.

Sutter rolled his shoulders as if loosening his muscles for a fight. "I have a hunch he does. I've called his aunt. She's expecting us."

Genna went to the bedroom to freshen her lipstick and retrieve her purse.

"You will be careful, won't you, Sutter?" Meredith clamped her teeth into her bottom lip. "I mean, you won't confront him, or... or make like a hero from the comics, will you?" She managed to put a cynical twist to the question, but she felt cold inside.

"Don't worry about me."

Sutter had shut himself into his cage again, allowing no one to question his actions.

"You were always one to meet a problem head on," she reminded him, a hard note coming into her voice. "With a psychopath, that might not be wise."

"She's right," Genna said, returning with her purse over her arm. "If we alarm him, he might do something desperate."

"Such as?" His voice was chipped ice, making it clear he'd deal with whatever situation arose.

"Guns make a nice loud statement," Genna mentioned quietly. "Let's talk to his aunt. With a history of his psychosis, we'll know more about dealing with him."

"Do you think he's violent?" Meredith demanded. "He must be, or else he wouldn't be doing this to Linda."

"Obviously he's very troubled," was all Genna would say. "We'd better be off."

They left Meredith to pace the narrow deck and worry. T.C. rubbed against her legs, making some comforting kitty sounds. She picked him up and stroked his fur. He licked her chin.

"You have fish breath," she teased, but her smile wobbled.

Meredith was relieved when Sutter and Genna finally returned late that afternoon. She'd envisioned them running into Fisher at his aunt's house and a fight ensuing. Not that Sutter would have lost a fair fight, but fists didn't stand a chance against a gun.

"Hello," she called, hauling herself aboard the boat, then pulling a terry-cloth robe over her bathing suit.

She'd found it impossible to work that morning. She'd chatted with Terry at the marina office and told her father of the latest developments when he'd returned, then she'd waited, occasionally swimming to pass the time.

After blotting the water off her legs, she followed Genna and Sutter into the cabin, where her father watched a baseball game on TV. He turned the set off. "How'd it go?" he asked.

"Is the guy dangerous?" she chimed in.

"Probably," Genna said, scanning her notes.

"Fisher has had a hard life," Sutter told them. "He was abandoned by his parents and taken in by a resentful relative—"

"His aunt didn't want him?" Meredith was at once sympathetic.

"Apparently not," Genna said. "But it takes more than a hard life to ruin a person. Lots of people have terrible childhoods and manage to grow up into decent human beings; in fact, that's the norm rather than the other way around."

"That people grow up okay?" Sutter asked.

"Yes."

"It doesn't sound that way in the newspapers."

Genna sighed. "I know. The sensational story sells papers, but they should be made to present a balanced picture. Sometimes the violent view of the world becomes a self-fulfilling prophecy."

"What do you mean?" Sutter gave Genna his Grand Inquisitor stare, guaranteed to extract the truth, no matter how painful.

Meredith twisted her hair into a towel and wrapped the ends turban-fashion around her head. She noted the tension in Sutter even as he leaned against the counter as if totally relaxed. His face was impassive, but his hands were concealed in his pockets as if to prevent them from giving away his feelings.

Genna thought before answering. "Well, take violence in the home. The popular press has written so much about abusive people having abused childhoods that everyone thinks it's a proven fact."

"That's what I've read," Richard put in.

"When we look into the backgrounds of abusive people, we find about three-fourths of them do come from violent situations, but that doesn't account for the one-quarter who don't. Also, of the children raised in such homes, only one child in four adopts a pattern of violence in reaction to frustration and anger.''

Sutter shot the psychologist a skeptical glance.

''It's true,'' Genna insisted. She shook her head sadly. ''It takes so little to save a child in that environment—the love of just one person, a parent or sibling, a teacher or counselor, even a friend the same age... just one person who can form a warm, caring bond with the child.''

Meredith turned her head and stared across the river as tears pressed against her eyes. It seemed so terrible to lose a child due to lack of love. ''So this person, Fisher, had no one to love him?'' she questioned in a throaty voice.

Sutter gave her a hard, knowing smile. ''Meredith adopts all strays,'' he said, looking at the wharf cat that lay on the deck in the sun.

T.C. opened his eyes and gave Sutter a disdainful cat stare, as if he knew what the man had said and wasn't bothered by it in the least.

''Oh,'' Genna exclaimed in annoyance, ''I've gotten off track. Violence in response to anger or frustration is a learned response. With proper training, a person can regain control of the emotions.''

''But it's not that way with an obsession?'' Meredith asked.

''Not without a lot of help.'' Genna studied her notes with a worried air. ''Fisher is probably dangerous.''

''How can you tell?''

''He's moved out of his aunt's home. They had an argument over a gun he bought a few weeks ago. She doesn't know where he is.''

Meredith gasped with alarm. ''A gun,'' she murmured, thinking of Linda. The secretary had been right to be afraid.

"What happens now?" Richard asked.

Sutter spoke, "We're getting Linda out of town...with no traces of where she's gone. That's why Genna and I are late getting back. We went to the office and made arrangements." He looked at his watch. "She should be getting on a plane about now."

"Now?" Meredith asked.

"We didn't even let her go home and pack in case he was watching. Thank goodness the nature of the work at CNI requires a security system. With that in place, we can screen everyone who tries to get in."

"He...he might try to get at you," Meredith pointed out.

The look of a warrior came over Sutter—fierce, undaunted and as dangerous as his enemies. "Let him," he said. "I can take care of myself."

Sometimes talking to him was like talking to a stone wall.

The week flew by. Meredith or her father piloted the houseboat along the delta. She took hundreds of water samples.

"What will you look for when you test these?" Genna asked late Friday afternoon when they again returned to their home port.

"Known carcinogens, industrial wastes, agricultural runoff. Salt." Meredith waved goodbye to the university student who'd met them at the dock and exchanged the filled samples with empty containers. Leaping back onto the houseboat, she rubbed her shoulders, then stretched her tired muscles.

"Because of the drought, cities have been taking water out of the delta, forcing bay water to come in and fill the void," she continued. "People with high blood pressure, heart disease and such are put at higher risk because of salt intrusion."

"Meredith!"

She glanced around. "Hi, Terry," she called to the marina manager. He ran with perfect ease along the floating dock. Genna grinned and went inside the cabin to give them privacy.

"Glad I caught you," he panted. "I'm off at six. I thought we might have dinner at the inn. The band has a new soloist who's really good."

Since no one had mentioned her birthday, she was at loose ends. "Sounds like fun."

"About eight?"

"Great."

He returned to business when a boat pulled up at the gas pump. She went into the cabin. Her father was in his room, taking his daily nap. The shower was running; Genna, obviously must be in there.

Meredith got a cola from the fridge and listened to the news on the small television. The world was in terrible shape. When Genna came out of the bathroom, Meredith decided she'd better get ready for her date. At seven-thirty, she came out of the bunk room.

Her father whistled. She did a pirouette for his and Genna's inspection. All that paddling about in the water had strengthened her hips and thighs, and she filled out her beige linen slacks better than she ever had. A silk turquoise top floated over her, outlining her breasts, the belted waist defining every curve.

"That color is perfect on you," Genna praised.

Meredith struck a pose. "I feel quite glamorous." With a rush of emotion, she hugged her father, then her friend. "Thank you both for the presents."

The blouse was a gift from Genna. The diamond earrings and pendant were from her father. They'd been waiting on her bed when she got out of the bath.

"I thought everyone had forgotten my birthday."

"Actually, we were planning on taking you out to dinner," her father said. "I'd made reservations earlier. I guess I should have consulted with the guest of honor. Genna told me you have a date."

"We can all go together."

"Terry might not want company," her father suggested with a wry smile. "I wouldn't have at that age." He glanced at Genna. "Maybe not at any age."

Meredith tossed her heard. The curls brushing her shoulders through the silk felt sensuous. "It's *my* birthday. I get to choose who I want to attend, and I choose you two."

And that ended the discussion.

If Terry felt any disappointment, he hid it well when he arrived for her. The four of them walked over to the restaurant together and were soon at ease. After dinner, Richard and Genna went off to talk to other friends they'd made along the delta.

"It's wonderful how relaxed and friendly everyone is on the river," Meredith commented. "Is it always this way?"

Terry, his gaze openly filled with admiration, nodded. "Most folks are on vacation. No schedules. No meetings. No reports to get out. It's easy to enjoy yourself."

"Even working, I find it pleasant. There's something about being on the water."

"Shall we dance?" he asked when the band started up.

They were among the first on the floor. As usual, the band went from a fast opening number to a slow one without pause. Terry put both hands at her waist. She laid hers on his shoulders, close, but not intimate. They talked, then fell silent.

That's the way they were when she spotted Sutter leaning against the bar, watching them. He was dressed in dark slacks and a dress shirt, the sleeves rolled back on his forearms. He met her eyes without smiling, then raised his glass to her.

"Happy birthday," he said.

She read his lips. "Thanks," she murmured.

"What?" Terry asked.

"Nothing. Shall we return to the table?"

Sutter reached it at the same time she and Terry did. She made the introductions. Sutter pulled out a chair and seated himself without waiting for an invitation.

"I've ordered champagne," he said, looking around with a frown. The waiter rushed over with the bottle already in an ice bucket. He placed three glasses on the table. "There'll be two more," Sutter told him.

"Yes, sir." The young man dashed off.

"Such an air of command," Meredith muttered.

Sutter looked at her. His grin was sudden and brilliant. "I gave him a big tip."

"What are we celebrating?" Terry wanted to know. He was doing well at hiding his chagrin at Sutter's arrival, but his smile looked a little crimped at the corners.

"Meredith's birthday," Sutter replied. He pulled a package from his pocket. "Here." He laid the gift on the table in front of her, thus staking a claim that went beyond Terry's.

She laid the unopened package in her lap, wariness creeping along her neck like an icy hand. Perhaps she was imagining it, but she sensed a tension in Sutter that reminded her of a cat about to spring. "Thank you," she said, "but you shouldn't have bothered."

"I've always brought you a present," he countered. "Since you were fourteen."

She turned to Terry. "Sutter is an old family friend."

The younger man visibly relaxed as she put Sutter into his proper place in her life.

"Not that old," Sutter murmured.

He gave her a sardonic smile when she glanced at him. The icy fingers stroked along her back. He seemed in a strange mood tonight. She remained silent while the waiter set two more glasses on the table and opened the champagne bottle.

Her father and Genna's return broke the tension of the moment. "Sutter," Richard exclaimed, holding out a hand, "we weren't expecting you."

Sutter stood and returned her father's handshake. "I couldn't miss Meredith's birthday," he said laconically.

"Glad you could join us. Ah, champagne. Meredith's favorite." Richard beamed at Terry.

"He ordered it." Terry waved a hand at Sutter.

The evening, which had started off on a congenial note, quickly deteriorated into discord, although not a cross word was spoken. Sutter, with cool charm, outshone the younger man without half trying. Meredith was furious with him.

Finally, Terry looked at his watch. "Listen, I have to check in at the store now. May I see you tomorrow?"

"Sure. We'll be here all morning." Meredith gave him a warm smile, friendlier than she really felt toward him. Blast Sutter.

"Great." He leaned over and kissed her cheek, then left.

"Well, what was that all about?" Richard demanded. "Why did he leave?"

"Sutter was being nasty," Meredith said coolly.

"Moi?" Sutter demanded with an air of shocked innocence.

"You made him feel as if he'd intruded on a family thing when you were the one who butted in. Here. I don't want this." She gave the present back to him.

"Aren't you going to open it?"

"No." She stood. "I'll see you two in the morning." With that, she walked out.

Sutter followed along behind her.

At the boat, she turned. "Isn't it enough that you spoiled my evening? What do you want now?"

"He wasn't much of a man if he couldn't stand a little competition," Sutter snorted.

"A braying donkey is competition?"

He slid his fingers around her neck and pulled her mouth close to his. She gazed up at him, defiant to the end. "I didn't think I handled it that badly," he murmured, staring at her mouth. He licked his lips as if he wanted to take a taste.

"Why, Sutter, are you vying for my favors?" She smiled with fake coyness while maintaining an outward calm.

"You chose the lover," he reminded her.

She was afraid to breathe in the sudden quiet that followed that declaration.

He released her and thrust the box into her hand. "Here. If you don't want it, throw it overboard."

She sighed and let the anger and the thrill of challenge seep out of her blood. Going into the cabin, she flicked on a lamp and opened the slender package. A tennis bracelet sparkled up at her.

"Are those rhinestones?" she asked dubiously.

"What do you think?"

She'd known they were diamonds. "I can't accept this. It's too expensive."

"Your father gave you diamonds."

"That's different." Her heart cracked a little. Didn't he understand that diamonds were a gift of love, of engagement?

He stalked the narrow space of the cabin. "Do what you want with the damned thing. I swear, a man can't even give you a simple birthday gift anymore."

"I don't want diamonds." She placed the gift on the table.

"Do you know what you want? Do you?" he demanded when she didn't answer.

An imp of mischief, with no care for survival, prompted her to say, "Yes. I'll take you as my lover for one year for my birthday gift. You'll have to give up your city woman, though."

He whirled on her. "What city woman?"

"The decorator, Beryl Somebody-or-other."

"She's nothing to me," he informed her.

Meredith poured a glass of water and took a drink, her fingers trembling as she tried for a casual air. "That's not how the newspaper article made it sound."

"She's not my woman."

"Who is?" She gulped a swallow of water and nearly choked. Portrait of a sophisticate, she mocked herself.

Sutter walked to the door. "No one." He went out.

Meredith followed and took a seat in the shadow of the awning. Sutter sat on the side of the boat, his thigh close to hers. He lifted her face to the slanted moonlight falling on the deck.

"Do you really want the position?" he challenged in an almost inaudible voice.

She pretended a casual indifference. "Maybe. What're the perks?"

"All the loving you can stand, any time of the day or night," he stated bluntly. A picture leaped into his mind—Meredith leaning over him, her breasts tempting him; him reaching up and taking one taut nipple into his mouth; her settling over him, taking him into her warmth, taking away the cold no fire could ever dispel. . . .

His fingers caressed her chin, then slid to her ear to rub the lobe between his thumb and forefinger. He toyed with the small diamond while waiting for her to answer.

"I'll take it. When do we start?"

Sparks blasted his body from inside at her bold declaration, lighting fires everywhere. His willpower was stretched to the limits while he fought the fever in his blood. She held his gaze for a heartstopping minute before looking away.

He checked the pulse in her neck with a hand that trembled with the need to touch her intimately. "You're not near as calm as you'd have me believe."

"Neither are you."

"Hell, I'm not calm at all. For two cents, maybe less, I'd haul you off to the bunk bed and show you what two creative people can do in a limited space if they put their minds to it."

"I've already given you the two pennies."

"You like to issue the dare, but would you care for the joust, I wonder?" He let his hand glide downward until he found her breast. He sucked in air on a quick breath. It burned clear down to his toes. "Are you wearing a bra under this top?"

"Of course I am." Meredith could hardly speak as he stroked a hot circle around the tip. Her nipple jutted against the cloth, aching for more.

"You always react like that. I've noticed."

"You stare at me . . . there."

"Come here," he muttered hoarsely.

He pulled her upright, then he was against her, pushing her back the one step that brought her up against the bulkhead. He held her trapped with his body while his hands clasped her head to position her for the kiss that was coming as surely as the sunrise would come with the dawn.

She couldn't stop the little croon of ecstasy that throbbed in her throat.

"Yes," he whispered, "sing for me."

His lips caused storms of sensation on hers. His hands roamed her body like a wizard's spell, enthralling her.

They were completely surrounded by the night, and she forgot that, at the other end of the marina, her father danced with Genna, that people were laughing, eating, listening to music. As far as she was concerned, there were only the two of them, alone in their own magic world.

"What prompted this? Seeing me with Terry?" She gasped at the implication. "Are you jealous?"

Sutter raised his head to stare into her upturned face. The pale lights of the quay diffused softly through the netting. His eyes, used to the dark, swept hungrily over her. Jealous? Enough to fight a pack of jackals for her!

"Yes. Were you going to let him touch you like this?"

"Kiss me again, Sutter."

"My God," he breathed, "you are a glutton for punishment."

"Not punishment. Heaven."

A tremor cavorted through her, and she rubbed her hands over his shoulders, enjoying his strength. He reminded her of a fortress, his foundation thrust deep into the earth, steady and enduring. She moved her hands up until she could frame his jaw and ran her thumbs back and forth across his lips.

"Damn you, Meredith," he whispered hoarsely. "You make a man weak just by looking at him."

"Do you always have to be strong? For just this moment, can't we be...vulnerable together?"

"No!"

He pulled her hands off him and walked away, standing with his back to her, his breath heaving in and out of his chest, as if the few steps he'd taken to separate them had been an Olympic race.

Pushing away from the wall, she went to him and twined her arms around him, her cheek pressed to his back. She rubbed against his shirt, a wanton, sensuous lethargy stealing over her.

"Make love to me," she whispered.

He shook his head.

"Then tell me why you won't."

"You were always a precocious kid." He laid his hands over hers, stopping their restless caresses, then he began guiding her movements over his chest, showing her how to stroke down, then back up the middle of his torso, making a circuit like two currents merging and flowing upward against all logic.

"Not really." She kissed him through the silk. "I'm still waiting for you."

He stiffened and grew very still, then he lifted her hands and turned to face her. "What are you saying?" he demanded, his voice thick with passion or rage, she couldn't tell which.

"You know," she accused softly and planted a kiss in the V of his shirt, then plucked at the wiry dark hairs with her lips.

"You can't still be a virgin, not after living in the city for all these years."

"I can prove it." She tilted her head and shook back her hair to gaze into his shocked, incredulous face. "Teach me to please you," she coaxed.

With a groan, he closed his eyes and crushed her against him, his large hands sweeping all over her, along her spine, her hips, over her buttocks and thighs, returning only to start again.

He kissed along her temple, avoiding her eager lips. "Tell me how to please *you,*" he whispered, a wildness in his voice and his hands.

When he moved, it was to brace her once more against the bulkhead and hold her there with the binding force of his masculine desire, clearly outlined against her. She moved against him and wrung a gasp from both of them.

She felt his hands against her waist, his fingers moving, unfastening the belt, slowly drawing her blouse upward. The material brushed against her sides as it rose, tantalizing her. She was heavy with the passion that bloomed within her. Unable to stand against its weight, she collapsed against him.

His hands slipped under the silky folds and along her sides. He touched her breasts, and his breathing became as ragged as hers. With slow, gentle movements, he insinuated his thighs between hers, lifting and supporting her between his body and the wall.

"Move against me," he ordered, sliding his hands to her hips to guide her before returning to cup her breasts.

She cried out at the sharp rasp of pleasure, then moved without his guidance. Against his softly exploring lips, she murmured, "I love your warmth, your arms...and hands, feeling you with all of me...touching me, touching you..."

"Shh." Sutter inhaled deeply, taking her scent far into himself, to a place where he'd never forget it. Inside, the cold receded a little, leaving him open to her, vulnerable.

He didn't like it, but he couldn't pull away. He'd wanted her too long.

He hovered over her for a second and blew against her lips, cooling her hot, demanding mouth with his breath. It was hopeless. He bent his head to hers for another kiss.

Meredith cried out, wanting him with a fierceness that left her shaken and throbbing all over. The longing exploded into uncontrollable fires within when he kissed her again. She twisted and pushed against him, his hips moving in perfect time with her rhythm, stoking the flames until she trembled from head to foot.

Suddenly, she gasped and went still. The magic flames poured over her, then froze into one gigantic surge of sensation. Her breath departed in a whoosh, and she was left spent and panting.

Sutter's muscles contracted into ropelike bands of steel under her hands as she held on to him for dear life. He thrust wildly against her... once, twice... and was still.

She felt the hard throb of his body against her, and the touch of his cheek against her temple as he rested. His heart raced in a primitive beat of spent passion and gradually slowed.

He stepped back, releasing her from the reckless captivity of his body. She watched him, knowing the aftereffects of splendor glowed in her eyes. And knowing she couldn't do a thing about it.

"Was that what you wanted, Meredith?" he asked.

He sounded weary, even defeated. She wanted him to feel the wonder that still coursed gently through her blood. "Part of it," she admitted. "It was wonderful, being close like that."

"Yeah," he said cynically. "Sex can be great."

"Was that all it was?"

"What else?"

"I don't believe that. We've shared too much, Sutter."

"I don't need this. I never asked for this." He ran a hand through his hair in an angry motion.

She hesitated when he moved away, then said, "Maybe it's a gift. You don't have to ask. It's a gift to us—"

"What?" he demanded, rounding on her. "Love? Is that what we're talking about?"

Even without light, she could discern the cynical curl of his mouth. "It could be." She was cautious, knowing how vulnerable she was to him.

"Love is a commodity that's often talked about. It's part of the psychobabble of the times."

"But you don't believe in it?"

He laughed briefly.

She chose her words carefully. "Someday you'll meet someone, Sutter, and your feelings for her will be so overpowering, you'll forget all these doubts."

"You've taken up fortune-telling?"

"No, but I know you. You have a great capacity for love, if you'd only let yourself see it. Did some woman hurt you?"

He was silent for so long she thought he wasn't going to answer. "No." He crossed the deck and stepped onto the quay. A draft of icy air, like the passing of a troubled spirit, remained in his place.

At his car, he paused, looking her way, but she knew he couldn't see her in the dark under the awning. She stepped onto the quay, into the pale-silver light of the moon and waved. After a second, he waved back.

After he'd driven off, she contemplated his gesture. There had been something terribly final in that farewell. The cold invaded her heart. Whoever Sutter might someday love, she knew it wasn't going to be her.

Chapter Six

Sutter hit the button when his intercom rang. "Yes?"

"A special delivery for you," his new secretary said. Her name was Carol and she'd been moved up from the steno pool on Monday. For some reason she seemed nervous around him and had yet to call him by name, although he'd told her to do so twice.

"Bring it in. Never mind, I'll come and get it," he decided.

He dropped the report on his desk, got up, stretched his back and went out. He'd faced one crisis after another at the office and had been putting in sixteen-hour days since last Saturday. Today was Thursday and there was no relief in sight.

Yesterday, he'd opened Linda's apartment for the Goodwill people to remove her furniture and clothing. When it was empty, he'd paid the building superintendent to have it cleaned. That had ended that episode. He hoped.

He walked into the secretary's office. "I'm going to lunch now. I'll work out first, so it'll be a couple of hours before I get back."

"Yes, sir."

"Sutter," he said, a little sharply.

"Sutter," she repeated like a schoolgirl, handing him the package with a shy smile.

He hoped she wasn't going to get a crush on him. That had happened with his first secretary, before he'd found Linda, and it had proven damned awkward.

Realizing how conceited he sounded, he smiled grimly. A dose of Meredith's cool barbs would cure him of any narcissism. If he ever saw her again. Since that hot episode on the boat—he got all heated just thinking about it—he'd vowed to keep his distance. They were too volatile together.

Going into the hall, he tore open the package, wrenching his mind back to the present and wondering what fire he'd have to put out next. Management by crisis was not his way of doing business.

He pulled out a single sheet of paper, read the one sentence written on it and stopped in his tracks. He spun around and headed for the security office.

"Is he in?" he snapped at the secretary upon entering.

"Yes, I'll tell—"

"Never mind."

Sutter strode into his security chief's office and closed the door behind him. He crossed to the desk and tossed the special-delivery envelope onto the cluttered surface.

Ned Barker, sixty, a veteran of two wars, clear-eyed and cool-thinking, held up one finger to indicate he'd be through with his caller in a minute.

"I'll check with you later," Ned said into the telephone and hung up. Without wasting words, he pulled the note from the envelope and read it, frowned, and read it again, aloud, "You took my woman, now I'll take yours."

"Three guesses," Sutter offered without a trace of a smile.

"Our friend, Fisher."

"Right." Sutter paced the floor. "Meredith has to have twenty-four-hour protection until we can figure out how to deal with this guy." His eyes darkened. "I know how I'd like to deal with him."

"I was just talking to the police chief," Barker told him. "They've run the checks. Fisher has no record. In school, he was a poor student but caused no trouble, as far as we can tell."

Sutter settled on the arm of a chair and stared out the window. "She'll have a fit, but what else can I do?" he asked in the tones of a reasonable man who'd argued his point for hours. "She'll just have to accept my decision on this."

"You want me to put a guard on her?"

Sutter nodded. "Your best man. He'll have to stay on the houseboat until she finishes her sampling."

"How long?" Barker asked.

"Another week, I think." He slammed a fist into his hand. "It was my fault. I didn't think..." The frown deepened between his eyes as he leaped to his feet. "I led Fisher right to her. I've got to get out there before—"

"Wait a minute," Ned called to Sutter's back. When Sutter stopped and turned, he said, "We'll need a list of all the women you've seen—all you've been seen *with*—before we can figure out who this psycho is talking about."

"I haven't dated in months, not since Meredith called me from the hospital," he admitted. "I've gone to the houseboat a dozen times...hell, I delivered her into Fisher's hands."

Ned cleared his throat, his manner sympathetic. "Sit down," he encouraged. "Let's plan this operation out. We don't want to overlook anything."

Sutter returned to the arm of the chair while they decided exactly how to handle the situation. When he rose, he was satisfied. There was room for an extra person aboard the houseboat. CNI's most trusted man could live there for the rest of the month and keep an eye out for Fisher.

"Are you crazy?" Meredith demanded, stubborn anger flashing from her hazel green eyes. "We don't need a strange man living with us. We're not even docked at a marina during the week. No one could slip—"

"Talk to her," Sutter demanded. "Maybe you can make her see reason."

Her father laid a comforting hand on his former protégé's shoulder. "He may be right," he told Meredith.

"I doubt if this Fisher guy knows I'm alive."

"He knows," Sutter cut in, his voice like ice shards. "I've been meeting you at least twice a week, sometimes more, when you dock. It'd be a simple thing to tail me."

"Nothing's happened so far, and we've been on the delta for three weeks," she reminded him.

"Fisher could rent a boat and follow us up one of those shallow sloughs you've been working in," Richard said, trying to figure out the logic of a madman's mind. "Since he has a gun, it would be a simple matter to get rid of both of us, especially since there's often no one else around."

Sutter faced Meredith. "He could ask at the marina like I did. Your friend, Terry, didn't hesitate to show me what area you said you'd be in. I found you without a problem."

"That's because I called him and told him to show you where we were on his big map when you insisted on coming." She gave him a questioning glance. "Besides, how do you know Fisher didn't follow you this time? He might be heading this way right this minute—"

"I can take care of him."

She saw him lift a hand to his side, then drop it. "You have a gun," she said, fear jarring her composure.

"Brilliant deduction," Sutter said with a hard smile. "You'll either accept the man I'm sending out for the rest of the month, or you'll get me. I'll sleep in the rental boat, if I have to. Which will it be?"

The power craft he'd rented was tied up at the back of the houseboat, its twin engines gleaming in the sun. It looked like something out of a James Bond movie.

"What do you think?" she asked her father. "The guard would have to sleep out here on the sofa."

Dr. Lawton shrugged. "A little inconvenience is a small price for peace of mind."

Sutter's peace of mind didn't particularly interest her. The couple of times he'd called during the past week, he'd asked for her father without wasting one word on her. She personally doubted Fisher would waste his time with her, either. The note was just a way of getting his own back at Sutter for helping Linda escape.

A chill suddenly washed over her. She rubbed the goose bumps from her arms. "Well, it certainly makes for an exciting life," she conceded. "Who is this guardian angel who's going to protect us?"

"John Barnard. He's one of the best," Sutter said with a nod of approval. "Barney worked with Genna on the personality profile and knows the most about Fisher. Fisher is devious. We don't think he'll attack with two men on board."

"That relieves my mind," she commented dryly.

Sutter swung a chilling gaze at her. "Don't go off without Barney. He's bringing a dory for you to do your sampling. That way, it'll look natural, like you're a team working on this project. When you return to town, there'll be a guard posted at your apartment—"

"No one's going to live with me," she stated.

A flicker of emotion whisked through his eyes. "We'll talk about it later."

"Right. Go for one victory at a time." She roamed around the luxurious cabin, stopping to remove a dying leaf from a violet or brush at a bit of dust, angry that she'd given in to having his guard aboard. "You might not always win, Sutter."

"Against you, I rarely do," he pointed out.

Their eyes locked. It wasn't until her father cleared his throat that they looked away.

She lifted the hair from her neck. "I've got work to do. When can we expect Rambo?"

"His name is John Barnard. He's called Barney," Sutter said bitingly. "He'll meet you at the marina tomorrow."

"Won't his family mind if he disappears for a week?"

"His kids are grown, and he was divorced years ago."

"I won't bother to ask why."

Sutter ignored her mocking comment. "I'll stay until then."

"Great," she muttered. She went outside and lowered a basket of sampling bottles onto the float. When she was ready to shove off and head up the slough again, Sutter came out to the aft deck.

He'd stripped to cutoffs and a long-sleeved shirt, open down the front. She stifled an impulse to lay her hand on his chest and sample the sensual feel of his hair against her palm.

"Where's your gun?"

"In this tackle box," he replied in the same sardonic tone. He moved toward the powerboat.

"You can't follow me in that monster. It'll stir up too much silt for me to get a true sample."

He grinned and stepped into the craft. He tossed an inner tube into the water, jumped after it and settled himself in it like a modern-day Huck Finn.

Meredith sighed and started off, Sutter paddling along behind her at a leisurely pace. She walked and pulled the float after her, stopping at every inlet to fill a bottle so they could discover what was running into the delta.

Actually, the floodplain was the junction of two great rivers, the Sacramento and the San Joaquin. Only a trickle flowed compared to the days before the dams and reservoirs had been built.

"I wish I'd been here," she murmured, "before the gold rush, before the dams, before all the people came in. Can't you just imagine the vast quiet of the plain, the awesome view of the snow-covered mountains on a clear day?"

Sutter looked toward the east, where a shimmer of haze kept the Sierras hidden. He thought of the men and women who'd traveled west to the golden land of California. Looking at Meredith, he saw a yearning so fierce and deep he had to glance away.

He was reminded of a mountain cat, its gleaming dark hair glowing with mahogany highlights in the sun, its eyes flashing green fire from their depths. There was something about her that was wild and sensual, as primitive as nature.

Without knowing how he knew, he realized she was a female ready to find her mate. There was a restlessness in her that went far beyond anything he'd experienced with a woman. He felt her need like a razor slash deep in his chest. It explained the loneliness he'd sensed in her. She needed a man of her own.

It was time. She was twenty-five. A woman...

His body hardened with a burning surge of raw male hormone, forcing him off his reclining position on the inner tube and into the water to cool off. It helped only a bit, and nothing helped the turmoil he experienced inside.

As if looking into the future, he saw her, laughing up at some man, whose face remained hidden. He saw the man lift her in his arms, hold her close to his heart, then carry her away. Sutter knew they were heading for a bedroom where the man would undress her and make slow, fierce love to her for hours. Meredith would give all her warmth to her lover, giving him everything he could ever dream of....

Realizing he'd stood still while she went on, he splashed forward. She cast him a questioning glance, then proceeded with her business. He wondered how she could concentrate when he was nearly out of his mind with a sex drive so powerful—

"You'll have to be still," she warned. "You're stirring up the silt." She stood quietly until the water had settled, then continued her work.

He remembered the little sounds she'd made last Friday. She hadn't been so calm then, he thought in satisfaction. In fact, she'd been wild in his arms.

When she bent to check the depth on the cord, it was all he could do not to wade forward and press his body to hers, to kiss the nape of her neck, bared when she'd tucked her hair under a brimmed straw hat before they'd started out.

Her mouth would be sweet...and welcoming. If he kissed her. He had to think of something else. He was supposed to be protecting her.

After scanning the area, he smiled, pleased. It would be damned hard for anyone to sneak up on them in this flat, grassy marsh. There wasn't a hill or tree in a mile. He went back to watching Meredith.

Her one-piece bathing suit somehow managed to look as skimpy as the bikinis she wore. The dip in the back went right down past her waist, and the material at her legs was cut high. It had nearly driven him over the edge, just thinking about how easy it would be to move that scrap of material aside and explore that womanly softness.

It was four tormenting hours later before she called it a day. He'd had to fight his natural impulses the whole time and decided he was apt to walk in a permanent stoop if he didn't get control of himself. The long trip back to the houseboat relieved the tension only partly.

Once there, he helped her unload her float and store the baskets in a locker. When she started to climb up, he held out a hand to her. Too late, he recognized the mischief in her eyes. With her feet pushing against the swim-out for leverage, she pulled him in, head first. He came up spluttering.

She swam around the boat. "Come on," she challenged. "You've been a grouch all afternoon. Let's relax before dinner."

The need for a small revenge overcame his better sense. He rolled into position for the breaststroke and started after her. He let her make it twice around the houseboat before he overtook her. His hands closed around her waist, and he lifted her onto the swim-out platform.

"Captured," he said.

"Please, sir, have mercy." She shook back her wet hair.

Sutter leaned forward, knowing he was going to kiss her throat in spite of all his good advice to himself. He felt as if he were going down for the third time.

Hell, what could a man do when a woman made it clear she was ready, willing and able?

Meredith turned on her right side, lay there for thirty seconds, then flipped to her stomach. After another half minute, she sat up, wishing Genna was still visiting so they could talk.

She climbed down from the top bunk, pushed two combs in her hair to keep it off her face and went into the main cabin. Sutter was stretched out on the sofa bed, one arm flung over his head, the other under the sheet.

As silent as a cat, she glided out to the aft deck and settled in a cushioned lawn chair, her feet tucked under her.

Her thoughts kept returning to the moment when Sutter had bent toward her, his eyes revealing the deep hunger of a man for a woman. Then her father had called them to dinner.

End of episode.

But not the end of whatever it was that drew them together. A premonition caused a chill to race over her skin. She had a sense of Fate closing in, stalking them the way Fisher had stalked Linda, the outcome inevitable. She and Sutter—

"What are you doing out here?" he demanded.

He spoke quietly, but his voice struck her like a whiplash. He stepped out on the deck and closed the door behind him. He'd pulled on a pair of jeans and a shirt, which he'd not buttoned. He took the chair next to hers.

"Enjoying the night," she said.

The breeze eddied through the netting, caressing her in its passing. The rustle of swamp grass surrounded them, whispering of a thousand secrets hidden in the dark.

She propped her heels on the edge of the chair, her nightshirt hanging past her toes, and wrapped her arms around her knees.

"I'm sorry for getting you and Richard into this mess," Sutter murmured several minutes later.

"It wasn't your fault."

"It was."

She heard more than the fierceness of anger in his voice. There was also the guilt of a naturally protective man who felt helpless against an enemy who wouldn't come out and fight in the open. She hardened her heart against her own natural compulsion to comfort him.

"If you want to flagellate yourself, find another witness," she told him. "You'll get no sympathy here."

He ignored her outburst. "I wanted to make your life easier, not complicate it with lunatics seeking revenge."

"You complicate it just by breathing," she told him with a rueful laugh.

After a surprised silence, he spoke again, his tone deeper, huskier. "You were never shy about sharing your feelings."

"I never knew I had to be, around you."

"Until recently."

She laid her cheek on her knees and gazed at him. "I'd hardly call melting in your arms a subtle act."

He looked away. "You're ready for a mate."

A jolt like an electric shock ran along her nerves. Said like that, it sounded as if he thought she was ruled by nature or a tide of hormones rushing through her blood.

"What about you?" she challenged. "You didn't exactly push me away."

"Don't you think I know that?" he snapped. "I shouldn't have touched you."

"Why not? You said you had all the normal male instincts. Why do you fight so hard against them?"

He didn't answer.

"Tell me of your youth," she demanded. "Make me understand you. You know all about me—my past, my dreams, all the secrets of my heart. Tell me yours."

"I have goals, not dreams."

"All right. CNI was one of those goals. You told me about it, now tell me another."

"That's it. I want the company to be a success—"

"It is," she cut in. "Don't you want a son to pass the family business on to?"

"No." The word was like an ice shard in the warm night.

"Coward," she taunted, gently but with feeling.

"You haven't forgotten my views on marriage."

"No, but what I don't understand is why. Where's your sense of adventure? You usually love new experiences."

He crossed his arms in the stony posture of an affronted male.

"You've seen businesses start and fail; it's one of the main industries in Silicon Valley," she reminded him, "yet you weren't afraid to take a chance on yourself with CNI. So what's the big deal about marriage?"

He made a sound, of humor or irony, she couldn't tell, but it was bitter.

"I'm not asking for myself, but for you," she assured him. She'd accepted the fact that she wasn't the one for him three years ago, had cried about it, and had gotten over it. "Don't you want a mate, too?"

"No."

She sensed his drawing inward as she probed for information. Someplace in his soul was a hidden chamber that no one was allowed to enter. Until he let someone in, he'd forever be a solitary man.

"Liar," she chided, "you want me."

"For the moment," he admitted, giving her a hungry glance. "But you want a lifetime. I don't have that much to give."

"Why not? Why do you lock yourself away?"

Sutter abruptly stood. With his back to her, he pulled his shirt closed. Being alone with her in the dark made him think of bed and lying beside her, of touching her...of her touching him....

He remembered the glow in her eyes when he'd held her and kissed her. She was an adult, but she lived in a fairy tale, believing love could conquer all. Her life, except for the loss of her mother, had been sheltered.

Reality was raised voices in the night, the wearing away of love until the glow was gone. It could also be the sound of fists striking flesh. The second time his father had turned anger into action, his mother had grabbed her son and left.

His half brother had also been a violent man, killed in a barroom while arguing with one of his drinking buddies. Sutter still felt the waste of that life with an acute sadness. He'd loved his brother, but that love hadn't been able to save him. Love just wasn't enough in the modern world.

"Why, Sutter?" she asked again.

Damned persistent female! "Because," he said. He knew that wouldn't satisfy her. "I've seen what happens when people marry. As soon as the shine wears off, they begin to rub each other the wrong way. Then they divorce. I've decided to bypass the first step and thus avoid the last."

"No human can live a life completely alone."

"Maybe you can't, but I can. I have my work and . . . a pleasant social life. I don't need anything else."

Meredith almost smiled as he censored his words for her. He'd always considered her sensibilities, even when she'd asked him the most intimate questions about boys and relationships all those years ago. "A pleasant social life doesn't sound like much compared to a fiery passion shared with a best friend."

"I didn't exclude passion," he reminded her coolly.

"Sex," she corrected. "I don't think they're the same at all. Passion involves emotions. Sex is just . . . nerve endings."

"Like on your birthday."

"That was passion. Both times, three years ago and—"

"You innocent babe," he mocked.

"You're the innocent," she contradicted. "You don't know me or yourself half so well as you claim if you think there was no more involvement between us than hormones."

"No doubt you're going to review all the juicy details of my life and give me some helpful hints on my true nature."

"No. I'll not do that. But if you weren't so all-fired determined to be the one man who's never needed anyone else, you would admit life is more fun, and troubles are halved, when shared with someone."

"The Meredith solution—every man needs a wife." A thread of mocking amusement ran through the words.

"Everyone needs somebody. Even strong men like you." She laid her hand on his. "Don't waste your life. You have a lot to give . . . to some woman."

His hand turned and clasped hers. "What about you? Instead of worrying over your father's love life, and mine, you should be thinking of your own. It's time you were getting married."

Her heart contracted until it felt about the size of a walnut. She thought of lying next to him all night, of being able to touch him as she pleased. "Are you asking?"

He'd been studying their entwined hands; now his gaze jerked to hers. "You know better."

She shook her head. "I just can't picture you a coward. Who hurt you? I told you all my woes when I was growing up. Can't you tell me yours?" she encouraged.

He released her hand and paced, six steps over, six steps back. She rose, too, and stepped close to him.

"I don't have any woes, as you call them. No one has hurt me." He turned on her. "I'm the wrong man, Meredith. Quit offering yourself to me."

"How embarrassing to be so obvious," she murmured, not at all abashed. This was Sutter, her best friend. There was nothing they couldn't confide to each other.

He sighed in exasperation. "You little witch, I should know better than to argue with you."

She leaned against him, and he wrapped his arms around her, his cheek against her hair. He began to sway, rocking his torso back and forth to music only he heard, moving her to his beat. An answering melody stirred through her blood. She began to hum the tune to "Unchained Melody." Sutter joined in, singing so softly she could barely hear him.

The hunger in his voice, in his seeking hands, was incredible. It plunged straight to the lonely core of her, releasing a longing so great it tore her soul to shreds.

She quit humming and listened to his voice. It ran over her in liquid ripples of pain. *His* pain. It was his hunger, his uncertainty, his yearning that she felt even more than her own.

She tightened her arms around him, her heart aching for something they both needed and might never find. She sensed that until she understood him—this man without a past—they had no chance for future happiness.

Chapter Seven

Meredith stood ready with the rope. As soon as her father guided the houseboat into position, she and Barney, the guard who'd been with them all week, jumped to the quay and tied up. It was the last day of June and the end of the trip. It seemed significant that those things coincided.

She smiled at her superstitions. From the corner of her eyes, she spied a whirl of black. T.C. bounded toward her and latched onto her ankle. She stooped and picked him up. He licked her chin and as much of her face as she'd permit, then settled to purring in her ear, his broad head snuggled against her neck.

"What a lover you are," she crooned. "I know some other males who could take lessons from you."

"What does he do that's so impressive?" Terry demanded, coming down the wooden planking.

"Makes a person feel missed. He's obviously delighted to see me." She laughed as T.C. took a playful nip at her neck, then licked her again. He resumed purring against her throat.

A light gleamed in Terry's gray-blue eyes. "I'm delighted, too," he said. With a boldness she hadn't expected, he leaned forward and kissed her. "Welcome to the home port."

"Thanks." She turned back to the boat. "We're packed. As soon as we move our stuff to the car, you can check the houseboat. Here's the key." Removing it from her pocket, she handed it to him. Still carrying T.C., she stepped onto the boat.

"There's someone waiting for you," Terry mentioned.

Her heart lurched. "Oh?"

She glanced around. Sutter climbed out of the CNI van and came toward them. His hair shifted in the breeze, dark and shiny. He wore sunglasses, and his smile was white against his tan. He looked fit. Muscles moved in his forearm when he shook hands with her father and Barney.

"Any trouble?" she heard him ask.

Barney told him they hadn't seen hide nor hair of anyone all week. That was nearly the truth. Only a few diehard fishermen had appeared on the banks of the deeper sloughs.

She released the cat and went over to the men, feeling Sutter's eyes, behind his dark glasses, take in everything about her, from her sandaled feet to the thoughts in her head.

Everyone, including Terry, lent a hand in carrying luggage and her last cases of sampling bottles to Meredith's car and the CNI van. They were soon ready to go. Meredith looked at her father. She realized they hadn't discussed the end of the trip and what was to come afterward.

There was an awkward silence as they stood in the parking lot of the marina.

"Do you want me to come home with you?" Richard asked.

Meredith started to say yes, but the patient smile on his face caused her to pause. She understood he felt a parental duty toward her; however, he'd been around people for a month, and she was certain he longed for the quiet of his own place as she did.

"No," she said. She gestured to the two other men. "I think I have enough protection." She spoke to Sutter. "What are the travel arrangements?"

"You'll go with me in the van," he decided. "Barney can take your father home in your car. I'll stay with you until he returns, and he'll stay with you for the night."

She didn't argue. "See? All taken care of," she said to her father. She kissed him on his cheek, and they held each other for a minute. "It was a super month," she whispered over a terrible knot that formed in her throat. Tears burned the back of her eyes.

"The best vacation I ever had," he murmured, his voice as husky as hers. He gripped her shoulders in a hard embrace.

She drew back and looked anxiously into his eyes.

He tapped her chin with his finger. "Don't worry about me. I'm feeling better than I have in a long time." He paused. "I liked your friend Genna, too. I hope we'll see her again."

Swallowing the tears in her throat, Meredith walked arm in arm with him to her car. They kissed once more before Barney drove off. She turned to Terry. This farewell wasn't a problem. She held out her hand and thanked him in a brisk, almost businesslike manner for his help during their use of the houseboat. She handled the goodbye so deftly that it was over before he could mention seeing her again. She sighed in relief as she walked to the tomcat lying in the sun on a dock post.

"Well, fella," she murmured, rubbing behind one ear. "I'd like to take you home with me, but you're happy here."

He raised his head and gave her an unblinking stare.

"Cats are territorial animals," she said aloud, reminding herself of that fact. "You'd have to be a house cat at my place."

T.C. purred and closed his eyes in bliss as she scratched his head and neck.

"I'm not going to shut you up in an apartment. You don't have to worry about that. So...so have a long and happy life."

She turned and walked to the van, climbing in the front seat beside Sutter. He started the engine and drove off after giving her a probing glance.

Meredith waved to Terry, but her eyes were on T.C. as he watched them leave. Another solitary male. She glanced at the one behind the wheel, then at the cat again as they left the marina.

"I'm surprised you didn't bring the stray with you," he said when they were on the road.

"He wouldn't like being closed up."

Sutter cocked one brow in a sardonic expression. "What male does?" he questioned philosophically.

"I don't feel like fencing your barbs today," she told him and turned her head to look out the window.

She heard him mutter under his breath. Then, "You always get so damned attached to strays, then you get hurt when they take off."

"There was only one—that dog that had been hit by a car. Its owner was the paper boy. Naturally I had to give it back to him when I realized why the animal got so excited each morning.''

They fell silent on the trip back to the city.

She told him what exit to take off the freeway to go to the university. Meredith heard the strain in her voice and concluded it had been a difficult week for everyone. With a guard on board, no matter how nice and unobtrusive he'd tried to be, she and her father had been forced into an awareness of danger.

An odd feeling, Meredith mused, watching the city slide past the windows like a fast-moving film. During the past few days, she'd realized how protected her life had been. She'd never even thought about danger to herself, except for the most obvious—staying off city streets at night, not talking to strangers, et cetera. She found she didn't like being suspicious of people. It wasn't her nature.

They passed the turnoff to Genna's house. Meredith wondered how her friend viewed her week on the delta and speculated on the friendship between her father and the psychologist.

They'd enjoyed each other's company, and she was certain her father had gotten Genna's address and telephone number before they returned to the marina and Genna departed. Meredith hoped they would continue seeing each other, but she wasn't going to force them into each other's company. Now it was up to them.

''Oh, here's our street,'' she exclaimed.

Sutter, his mind evidently on other matters, successfully made the turn. Meredith directed him to the university building where they stored her samples in the lab. Then he drove the few blocks to her apartment complex, his eyes scanning the street and rearview mirror with the concentration of a warrior.

No one lurked behind a bush or tree as they walked up the path to her door. No one waited inside the silent apartment when they entered. No madman leaped out with a gun when she went into her bedroom to put her clothing away. She sighed in relief.

Sutter took her box of cleaning supplies to the kitchen. She joined him there. She glanced at him when she finished storing the items. "I need to go to the grocery store."

"I'll go," he volunteered. "What do you want?"

"I don't know." She began planning the week's menus. "What does Barney like to eat?"

"You won't be feeding CNI people," he informed her. "Dinner will be brought in every night from the company cafeteria for the security patrol, you included."

"How about now? Are you hungry?"

The air sizzled with an escalation of tension. She wanted him to say yes, to admit to the hunger between them, to sweep her into his arms and make love to her. Naturally, he didn't.

"No," he said. He walked out and closed the door behind him.

She went to the window and saw him climb into the van. He stayed there until Barney returned with her car and took up the task of keeping her safe.

The sound of footsteps prowling the apartment was driving her right up the wall. Meredith gritted her teeth and stared through the dark at the ceiling. For almost a week, she'd been awakened, heart pounding, by the sounds of Sutter's guards moving from window to window, checking for anyone loitering near her apartment.

During the day, someone was always with her—at the lab, at her place, or traveling between the two. She'd gone for pizza and a movie with two friends; Barney had to tag along. It had put a damper on the evening, and she'd made no more attempts to go out.

The only time she had alone was either in bed or in the bathroom. Even then, the guard was right outside the door.

One thing she could say for the three men Sutter had assigned to round-the-clock duty—they never relaxed their vigilance. She heard the creak of wood flooring as Barney moved to another position. And they never slept.

She flung her legs off the bed, but didn't get up. Where would she go? To the living room to watch TV? Barney would fade silently into another room unless she invited him to join her. If she did, every few minutes he'd get up to make his rounds again.

This was ridiculous!

She grabbed the phone and dialed Sutter's number. He answered on the second ring, his voice husky with sleep.

For a second, she imagined how he must look, his hair tousled, his torso bare as the sheet slipped down to his waist. Heat flooded her body in a tidal wave of desire.

"Meredith?" he inquired when she didn't speak.

"How did you know it was me?"

"Who else would call at . . . twelve minutes past midnight?"

"A sadist," she snapped. "I can't sleep with that guard in the house. This has got to stop."

"Is he bothering you?" A deadly quiet dropped like a hand grenade into Sutter's voice.

"Not the way you mean," she replied dryly. "It's just that I'm not used to someone else stirring around. It's driving me crazy. Besides, nothing has happened. Fisher hasn't been seen or heard from in ages. You're wasting your money."

"Let me worry about my finances."

"Yeah, but who's going to worry about my mind when I go stark raving mad?" There was silence on the end of the line. "Sutter?"

"I'm thinking."

She waited for thirty seconds.

"How about if I find a woman to stay with you? She could live there and sleep in the spare room. That way you wouldn't be disturbed at night."

"No. No more, Sutter. I've had enough."

Sutter heard the finality in Meredith's voice. In a way, she was right. There'd been no new developments in days. "All right," he said. "Have Barney call me in the morning. I'll call off the dogs . . . on one condition."

"What is that?"

He grimaced at the wariness in her voice. Once she'd trusted him so completely, he could have invited her to stay at his place until he got this mess sorted out, but now . . . now he had only to hear her voice and he went as hard as a marble column.

"Sutter?"

"Sorry, I was thinking of something," he said. "What are your plans tomorrow?"

"I'm going to start my report on salt intrusion into the delta. It's worse than we thought—"

"Tomorrow's the Fourth of July," he reminded her.

Meredith chewed on her lower lip. Her father had called earlier in the week and invited her to come down to watch the fireworks at Bayshore Park with him and Genna, but she'd declined. The young legislator she'd dated in the spring had asked her to an outing, but she couldn't face a day of politicking. After that, she'd forgotten all about the holiday as she became engrossed in her work.

"I'm going to start my report," she repeated.

He made an exasperated sound. "Come to the company picnic at the river park."

"I don't work for CNI."

"As my guest. That's the condition."

His tone dared her to accept his invitation, much the way she'd challenged him during their time together on the boat. There was something between them, something strong and elemental that gripped them both and wouldn't let go. "Thanks, but—"

"I'll be by for you around nine-thirty." He hung up.

"You won't always win," she said, slamming the phone down.

Her anger dissolved slowly. She laid a hand over her abdomen where her insides churned like a pan of water set to boil. Sutter was determined to hover over her—either in person or through his guards—and shield her from danger like... like a hen with one chick! Well, she was not his little nestling, and she was going to inform him of that fact! Her life had been disrupted all she was going to allow it to be.

Too restless to sleep, she sprang out of bed and went to the window. There, she pulled aside the curtain. Out on the street, a lone man walked under the orange glow of the streetlight.

She watched him, wondering who he was and what he was doing out at this hour. She glanced at the clock. The witching hour. Wrapping her arms across her chest, she wished she weren't alone.

She had to laugh, albeit silently. She hadn't been alone in over a month. What she really wished for, she couldn't have.

The doorbell rang promptly at nine-thirty. When Sutter entered, he talked to Barney first. A few minutes later, the guard left with a smile and a wave to her. Meredith lost no time in stating her grievances to Sutter.

"I know no one is watching me. I'd feel it if he were."

Sutter scoffed. "Women's intuition? I've never known anyone, particularly a criminal, to be predictable."

"Maybe not, but—"

Sutter caught her gesturing hand in his own warm clasp. "Don't argue with me today, Meredith. I've had a hell of a week."

"What's wrong?" She scanned his familiar features. He did look tired. The lines seemed deeper at the sides of his mouth, and a permanent frown scored a line between his brows.

He rolled his eyes heavenward. "Not a thing. We're just busting our butts getting a major bid together that could double our business if we win it, there's a nut sending me threats, and the IRS is questioning a credit deduction on our taxes. Other than those minor things, there's you."

"I haven't done anything," she said defensively, feeling herself softening toward him.

"You don't want guards in the house. You don't think anyone will hurt you. For heaven's sake, Meredith, wake up. This isn't a paradise you live in."

"You don't have to feel responsible for me—"

"Hellfire, I *am* responsible." He rammed both hands into the back pockets of his jeans. The action outlined the solid lines of his thighs and flat stomach.

Meredith clamped her teeth together and fought the restless need that rose to choke her. Perhaps it was the sense of danger, perhaps it was being near Sutter, but she could no longer be sure her emotions would obey her command.

"Sutter, I think I'd rather not go today. I promise to stay inside and work."

"No."

"Why not?" He was the most impossible person!

"I think you need to get out," he continued. "You've only been out once since you got off the houseboat."

She realized the guards must have reported her every move. Anger churned with the restlessness, and she paced across the room to stand at the empty hearth. Before she could voice her feelings, she noticed the expression on Sutter's face. Frustration, guilt, fatigue. The past weeks had taken their toll on him, too.

Biting back the sharp words, she went for her purse. "We'd better go. We don't want to miss any of the fun."

She smiled at his blank look of astonishment.

"You never cease to surprise me," he murmured, taking her arm when they went outside, his eyes skimming the area for trouble.

A frisson dashed along her back. Where he touched her, her skin seemed to glow.

"We're going to Old Sacramento first," Sutter said. "There's a train exhibit I thought you might like."

He knew she loved model trains. "That was thoughtful of you."

Now that they were on the road, they were almost formal with each other, like strangers on a blind date. He found a place on the street to park and scanned the pavement.

"See any weirdos?" she inquired with false sweetness.

He narrowed his eyes at her, framing the dark blue irises in coal black lashes. The wind ruffled his hair. His strength was a tangible force, coiled and ready for action like a bullwhip.

"Only one smart-mouth," he drawled, that tinge of Alabama accent softening the sardonic overtones.

They were the first ones in the exhibit hall when it opened at eleven. Two trains were already running on the elaborate track setup. One engine, its boxcars replicas of actual 1830 rolling stock, sent out puffs of steam just like a real one. A tiny fireman tossed wood into the furnace.

"What fun!" a woman behind them exclaimed, pushing past Meredith to the head of the line. Sutter frowned. Meredith laid her hand on his arm, quieting him.

The man behind the controls was delighted with the interest as the woman and Meredith gathered around his display. "These narrow-gauge trains are still used for vegetable harvests in some places. Would you like to play engineer?" He moved aside so the woman could get to the controls.

Sutter went to the window and peered outside before resuming his place next to Meredith.

"Surely you don't think anything could happen in the crowd that'll be roaming the streets today," Meredith remarked, leaning on the guardrail beside Sutter and watching the trains make another circuit through the "mountains" of the layout.

"I hope not," he said tersely. "But then, we don't know who'll be roaming the streets mixed in with the crowd."

She sighed and ran a hand through her hair. "Do you know what Fisher looks like?"

"Yes. My security chief got a picture when he was hanging around the street outside the gate."

"Do you have it?" she demanded. "Let me see."

Sutter took out his wallet and removed a photo. The young man who stared into the camera was thin, with hair that touched his collar and a skimpy beard and mustache that didn't hide the weakness of his mouth. There was something about him that seemed unformed, as if he'd stopped maturing long ago.

"He looks unhappy." She handed it back and moved off.

Sutter glanced at the photograph before putting it away. He didn't feel any sympathy. In his opinion, any man who would terrorize an innocent woman deserved whatever happened to him.

His gaze went to Meredith. She was watching the tourist and the train owner handle the controls. When the woman moved aside, she laughed and took over. Anger coiled like a viper in his stomach. That anyone would threaten her...

A strange feeling, part tenderness, part something else that he couldn't define, ran through him. Meredith was independent, she was as stubborn as a blasted mule when she made up her mind, and yet she was caring and generous to a fault. She was quick-tempered, but just as quick to sympathy.

He heard her chortle when her train overtook and passed the first one. Her laughter was just this side of heaven.

He clenched a fist. Anyone who hurt her would have to go through him. He glanced over the crowd that was getting denser with each moment. By midafternoon, they'd be hard put to squeeze through the mob. Hundreds, perhaps thousands of people milled around the shops and buildings in the historic district. The area was as clogged as he'd predicted it would be.

"I think we'd better go," he suggested two hours later as they exited an old-fashioned candy store.

"I'm starved," Meredith said. "The lines at the restaurants are horrendous."

"The picnic will be getting underway about now." He thought they'd be safer there. For one thing, his security people would be on hand. For another, a strange face in the crowd would stand out among his employees.

They returned to Sutter's car.

Sutter suddenly spoke. "Over there, to the right of the light pole. The guy with the cap."

Meredith stared intently toward the street corner. She spotted a glimpse of brown hair sticking out from a billed cap and shoulders covered by a black T-shirt before the man disappeared into the crowd.

"I couldn't tell," she said. "Circle the block. I'll see if I can spot him again."

"Get down," Sutter ordered. "I don't want him to see you."

She slid down in the seat until her head was lower than the windows. "I feel like the heroine in a spy movie."

A grin sliced across Sutter's face, and he gazed down at her for a moment. "Right."

Meredith smiled, at ease with her oldest friend for the first time that morning. "That kid wasn't more than sixteen if he was a day," she said. "I'm sure it wasn't Fisher."

Sutter ignored her while he drove around the block once more at a speed just short of a worm's pace. People darted across the street in front of the car without the slightest heed to traffic.

"No sign of him." Sutter sounded disappointed.

Meredith didn't talk on the way to the park. She was thinking of Sutter confronting a madman, one who had a gun. If something happened to Sutter...

It was unthinkable. He'd been the center of her life for years. He'd shaped her dreams and sparked the brilliance that made her days shine with a golden light. Yet he'd never permitted her even the memory of true fulfillment in his arms. In a flash of insight, she knew that when she learned all there was to know about sharing herself with a man, she wanted it to be with him, only him.

As if sensing her premature grief, Sutter took her hand and squeezed it before releasing her. "You can sit up."

At the park, Sutter opened the trunk to disclose two folded director's chairs. Taking her arm with one hand and carrying the chairs with the other, he headed across the lawn to a large group gathered under an alder tree next to the river. A valley oak gave a degree of privacy from another noisy group.

"Sutter, hey! Here comes the boss. Straighten up, guys." A young man shouted greetings and advice.

"Come on, serve. You're just ogling the boss's lady," a teammate called out.

"Got to check the scenery," the young man explained, his dark eyes running over Meredith in appreciation. "You gonna tell us who she is?" he asked Sutter. "Is she a new employee?" He gave her an interested leer.

She saw Sutter's dark blue gaze flick to her outfit—snug white jeans and a blue Hawaiian shirt with white flowers that tied at her waist—before he turned her toward a more sedate crowd around the barbecue grill.

"She's my date," Sutter told them over his shoulder.

"Ah, heck," the impudent young man said.

A smile curled the corners of Sutter's mouth, and his grip on her arm tightened briefly. Meredith tried without success to quell the riot in her veins. Sutter's date. She'd never been that before.

"Date?" she questioned in low tones before they joined the noisy bunch around the food.

He looked down at her, his eyes fathoms deep and just as mysterious. "Any objections?"

"No...." She thought of moonlight and parked cars. "Is this the first step to becoming lovers?"

He stopped.

"You do remember my birthday present, don't you?"

He looked at the bracelet on her wrist. "You're wearing it."

Before she could reply, Sutter was called to the grill. "You're supposed to help with the cooking," a well-muscled man with graying hair reminded him.

The man was introduced as Ned Barker, CNI's chief of security. Meredith met the treasurer, the corporation secretary, a couple of vice presidents and their spouses. She was pleased to see the treasurer and a VP were women.

In a few minutes, hot dogs were browning on the grill, tended by Sutter and the security chief. She spotted Barney in the crowd watching the volleyball game. Meredith sat in one of the chairs Sutter had brought and enjoyed the sight of all the activity.

When the food was ready, Sutter prepared a plate for Meredith and one for himself. He gallantly gave his chair to the treasurer and sat on the ground next to Meredith.

"Ah, a man who knows his place," the woman said in approving tones with a wink at Meredith.

"But it's very hard to keep him in it," Meredith replied.

Sutter looked up at her with a laugh.

At that moment, the world could have stood still. Their eyes met and held for a second that lasted to eternity. He looked away first, shifting his long, masculine body as if the ground were suddenly uncomfortable.

Meredith met the treasurer's curious glance and managed a smile. Could the woman detect the currents that ran between her and Sutter? The smile had faded from his face, and he concentrated on his food like a man at his last meal. She let her gaze roam over the picnic area.

The ritual of feasting, she mused. It feeds the body and the soul. "Good food, good company, good cheer..." She recalled an old toast from some forgotten book. It had been a while since she'd been on an outing like this. She'd forgotten what fun it could be.

"Thanks for bringing me," she said, leaning toward Sutter and gazing into his eyes.

He nodded, then blinked and turned away, his jaw taking on a hard edge.

Sutter wanted to tell her to stop it. She shouldn't look at him with her smile all warm, like honey ready to pour over him, as if she'd give him anything he asked.

Her giving was part of her, he realized. She never thought of holding back. Her love flowed outward like a warm brook and never seemed to need refilling. He wanted to give her a stern lecture on this.

Some man might take advantage of her. She might meet someone who didn't care for her the way he did.... Dammit, yes, he cared for her! He'd watched her blossom into womanhood. He'd seen her grow in wisdom as well as knowledge. Except where he was concerned.

She looked at him and saw something that didn't exist. She thought he had a goodness to match her own, but he didn't. Inside him was a dark place, as cold as his brother's grave.

He watched Meredith finish her meal and lick her fingers, then her pink tongue swiped around her lips before she wiped them with a napkin. He went hot all over like a poker stuck in a fire.

It was the taste of her that he craved and had for three years. She was right. That night was burned in his memory, and he couldn't discuss it because it seared his control right down to a sizzle of ashes. He hardly chewed the hot dog before he swallowed it, then gulped down the remainder of his soda. He needed more than that to put out the fire she caused.

"Look, there's someone in a boat," Meredith said, routing his heated thoughts. "That looks like fun. I wonder if there's any chance of renting one."

"We can check after we finish eating," he told her.

The young engineer who'd teased them when they first arrived drew Meredith into a volleyball game early in the afternoon. Sutter signaled to the guards to keep an eye on her while he reserved the boat. When he returned, he saw the engineer, Jim somebody, leap for the ball. He crashed into Meredith.

With an effort, Sutter held his tongue while Jim grabbed Meredith to steady her. The game proceeded. In a minute, though, the same thing happened. Again, Jim steadied her, his hands much too free on her body in Sutter's opinion. He clamped a lid on his temper. Meredith hated a scene.

The third time the engineer "ran" into Meredith, Sutter stepped forward. He'd had enough. He'd put a stop to this before the blockhead hurt Meredith. Before he'd gone three steps, Meredith's laughing voice rang out.

"Play your own position, you clumsy oaf," she told the young man, giving him a hearty shove away from her. "You get in my way again and I'll conk you."

"Yeah, you clumsy oaf, play your own position," several of the men jeered.

Sutter smiled as the young engineer's ears turned bright red. While Meredith had spoken in a friendly enough manner, the steel in her voice had told him she was aware of his shenanigans and didn't find them amusing. Sutter stayed on the sidelines until the game ended, then he moved forward to take Meredith's hand.

"Ready for that boat ride?" He was surprised to hear how husky his voice had become. He cleared his throat.

She looked at him with her soft hazel eyes. "We don't have to."

He couldn't tell if she wanted to go or not. Maybe she didn't want to be alone with him. Maybe she knew his gut was a burning ball of desire for her. With her face flushed and her hair in tangles on her shoulders, she looked like the all-American girl that every man dreams of.

His throat closed. If their lives were different, if he could give her what she wanted, what she deserved—

He stopped that line of thinking. Life was what it was. Nothing could change that.

"I want to," he said. "Come on."

They went to the rental dock and soon were on the water. Sutter rowed leisurely up the river, intending to let the gentle current bring them back.

"Umm, this is nice," she murmured. She put a cushion in the bottom and sat facing him. Positioning the life preserver against the edge of the plank seat, she used it as a backrest.

Sutter pushed harder against the oars after observing her lashes drop over her eyes to a sexy level. Bedroom eyes. Did she know?

He studied her closely, but she seemed merely relaxed, content to watch the shore drift past without comment.

"Do you want me to help?" she asked.

"No."

She lifted her lashes to study him. "That was a short answer. Are you angry about something?"

"No. Sorry, I didn't mean to sound snappish."

She continued looking at him. He shouldn't have brought her out here. Houses lined the river, so they weren't alone, but the sense of privacy was complete. There wasn't another boat within a hundred yards. He had her to himself, and it was driving him wild.

"Don't," he said when he saw her eyes flick along his body. She noted his dilemma and smiled, not a big smile, just a gentle turning of the corners of her mouth.

"You're...you...want me," she said in a dreamy voice.

He remembered how she crooned when he kissed her deeply and wanted to hear it now. He shrugged. "Watching you leap around during that game gave me...ideas."

She wrinkled her nose at him. Her smile became a grin. "It gave ideas to that buffoon on my team, too."

Sutter scowled. "Yeah. I started coming after him."

"Did you really?" She caught her lower lip between her teeth and gazed at him adoringly. "My hero."

He realized she was teasing him and felt the heat rise to his ears. Damned impudent female. "You're looking at the wrong man if you're looking for a hero."

She leaned back again and shook her head. "I don't think so. You've put yourself out to protect me, even though you're working on that bid for the big contract."

"Yeah, Sutter Kinnard, boy wonder."

"Hardly a boy," she corrected, her gaze sliding down him.

He put his back into besting the tug of the current.

They were silent for a while. She let her fingers trail in the river, then flicked the water at him. After a peaceful twenty minutes during which he imagined they were back to where they'd been years ago—their friendship simple and uncomplicated by desire—he heard her sigh.

"Why the heavy sigh?" he asked.

"I was thinking of my father and Genna."

"Does their relationship bother you?"

"No."

"Not even the thought of another woman taking your mother's place?" Would she be hurt if her father married again?

Meredith watched Sutter's powerful muscles move. "Genna will have a place of her own." She considered what he'd said. "Did you feel that way about your stepmother, that she was intruding?"

"No." His curt answer declined further discussion.

"Did you like her?" She saw his expression snap closed like a disturbed clam and knew she had encroached beyond his limits.

"Yes, I liked her. I still do."

Meredith was surprised. "Are they still married? For some reason, I'd assumed they weren't."

"There are some women crazy enough to put up with the Kinnard men. My stepmother is one."

"Maybe there's one who'll put up with you," she suggested, knowing her continued probing would only create hostility between them. "Maybe—"

"I haven't asked a woman to put up with me."

"Are the Kinnard men so hard to live with?" She smiled encouragingly at him, wanting him to confide in her.

"Yes."

"Why?"

"It's an old story and not very interesting." He swung the oars vigorously into the water and sent them zooming forward.

She could see the wall going up around him. "Tell it to me."

"You just never let up, do you?" He glared at her. "Here's the story. My father is one of those men who reacts to frustration with violence. When the anger reaches a certain level, he starts drinking... and uses that as an excuse to start hitting."

Meredith refused to be shocked. "Did he hit you?"

Sutter shook his head. "The women in his life," he said cynically. "If they stayed around and let him."

An idea dawned on Meredith. "You don't think . . . you surely don't think you'd be like that, do you? Sutter, you can't possibly think you'd be like that." She sat up, causing the boat to rock wildly from side to side.

Sutter cursed. "Be still."

"Do you?" she persisted.

"No," he said, his jaws so tight he could hardly talk. "I'd never hit a woman, or anyone if I could help it."

"I know," she said, and drove him senseless by gazing at him with all the confidence in the world in her eyes. She'd always thought he was some kind of perfect.

He stifled a groan, his blood going to boiling in a split second. He knew he was only a man, but when she looked at him like he was a damned hero, he wanted to perform great deeds. She could drive him wild with just a touch, a look, a glimpse of her pink tongue as she spoke. The fact that she wanted him just as much was no help.

She leaned her head back and studied him. "I'm sorry about your family. It doesn't have to be that way, though. When two people love each other, they can work through things."

He felt as if he'd just swallowed an artichoke . . . whole. Her eyes glowed like foxfire in the late afternoon sun, the radiance spiraling inside him, warming a place that had been cold for years.

"Love isn't enough," he heard himself say.

"Yes, it is. You just have to believe—"

"You live in never-never land."

"Where dreams come true," she finished in a husky voice.

The threads of longing stretched between them. She was as aware of them as he was.

"Genna was wrong," he told her, trying to explain. "Love doesn't work. I loved my father. So did my mother.

It didn't change anything. I loved my brother. His mother loved him. But her love wasn't enough to save him. He died, a useless, wasted death, for no reason.''

"You can't blame yourself. You were rarely with them, a few weeks in the summer—''

"I've seen what happens to other people who fall in love. It doesn't last. Nothing lasts.''

"Not even desire?'' Meredith asked softly. She wanted to keep him talking. She was near some fundamental truth about Sutter, if she could just reach it before he closed the door on her.

He gave a contemptuous snort.

"But we haven't tried it yet,'' she reminded him. She issued a direct challenge. "'Come live with me and be my love.'''

"And we will all love's pleasures prove?'' he paraphrased. "I'm long past the belief that love is a cure-all.''

A ripple like pain went through his eyes before he glanced away up the river. Meredith understood then.

In Sutter's experience, love didn't work. It had never been enough to create the life he'd longed for as a boy. Love hadn't changed his father or his brother. It hadn't brought happiness to the women who'd loved them. The bonds between people that should have been supportive and loving had been destructive and hurting, and he'd closed himself off from them.

Strong, brave and as tough as they come, Sutter was afraid to love.

Chapter Eight

Meredith watched the shore drift by, but her eyes were on a past she was just now beginning to comprehend. She saw Sutter as a boy, young and hopeful, confident that the force of his love would make everything all right. She saw him bury that love when his family fell apart.

She recalled how distant he'd been, how dark his glance, when he'd returned from his brother's funeral. But long before that, he'd built a wall around his heart, deliberately and carefully. Because it hurt too much otherwise.

He'd loved her family, but he'd kept himself outside it, too, insisting on a pretend sibling relationship that neither of them had felt in the least. And lately, by refusing to recognize anything deeper than friendship between them, he'd tried to keep them on safe footing.

It was like telling an apple to stay green. It couldn't be done. Her feelings for him had ripened into love as she'd grown into womanhood. And into desire, she acknowledged, the natural outcome of love. There was nothing she could do to prevent it.

But Sutter hadn't wanted her love or her passion. He didn't trust the first and was too honorable to take the second.

She pondered the situation while he rowed them back to the dock. When he took her arm to help her out of the boat, an electric current ran through her at the contact. She met his eyes and knew he'd felt it, too. He moved away from her.

"Ignoring it won't work," she said softly after he'd paid the dock manager and they were walking across the lawn toward his car.

"What?" He gave her a cool glance.

"Pretending the passion doesn't exist. It does. From the looks of things, it isn't going to go away." She raised her hair off her neck and let it cascade down slowly.

"Take a cold shower," he advised, lengthening his stride.

Nearby, a couple lay in the grass, deep in an embrace that would have embarrassed her to perform in public. Tears filmed her eyes, surprising her.

Sutter was right. She *was* going through a crisis. At twenty-five? By fifty, she'd be a basket case.

The feeble attempt at humor didn't quite come off. Something had to change between them, she realized. She felt she was at a crossroads that would forever determine her life course.

"'There is a tide in the affairs of men,'" she quoted, "'which, taken at the flood, leads on to fortune...'"

Sutter answered calls of farewell from the group still at the picnic tables. Meredith noted that the sun was almost setting and evening was drawing pastel colors across the sky. The day had gone so fast.

As fast as a life, she mused on the way home. Twenty-five. A third of her life by today's standards.

"You're quoting a lot of poetry lately," Sutter remarked.

"It seems to express what I feel."

"Such as?"

"Time passes. Things change. Life goes on."

They reached her apartment complex. He walked her to her door. "Feeling melancholy?" he asked, a smile touching his lips.

"Yes." She unlocked the front door and turned. "I want more from life than what I have."

Sutter turned from her and faced the west, where the sky had turned purple and magenta with edges of gold. "I know," he said. For a second, he looked as sad as she felt. He turned to her. "I want to send a guard over."

She shook her head.

"A woman who will live in—"

"No." She met his eyes. "I might consider coming home with you."

"Like hell."

"Why not?"

He was blunt. "You know what would happen."

She gave him an impudent glance in return for his hard one.

He leaned nearer to her, so close only a breath divided his lips from hers. "Just push me a little farther," he said in a voice of quiet menace.

"I'll have to. I'm not giving another inch."

He frowned. "What the hell does that mean?"

She didn't answer, but withstood his increasing ire long past the time her courage gave out. With the mulishness of desperation, she stared into the blue fury of his gaze. When she could stand it no longer, she closed her eyes and moved her head from side to side, denying his will over hers.

"A person can't talk sense to you anymore. You've gotten some fantasy in your head about us, and I don't know how to get rid of it." He gave a short bark of laughter. "Except maybe the standard caveman treatment."

Hands touched the sides of her face, stilling her movement. Then lips, warm, masculine lips, settled over hers.

She froze. With every ounce of willpower she possessed, she resisted him.

"Stop fighting me," he growled, nipping at her lips. Changing tactics, he ran his tongue over her mouth.

"I have to," she said. "You're trying to use my feelings for you to get your way."

He drew back as if stung. "I'm thinking of your safety. How could I face your father if I let something happen to you?"

He looked at her without moving. She slipped both hands around his neck and clasped them together, holding him captive.

"Unfair," she protested. "My weakest point—"

"Yes, your infinite capacity for love."

His words confused her, mocked her. She searched his eyes for meaning, but Sutter disclosed only what he wished to.

"Of course I love my father."

"Of course," he agreed.

He caressed down her arms and touched her waist. When she felt his hands glide upward, she went very still. He moved again, until his hands rested against the curve of her breasts. His mouth was once again close to hers, their lips almost touching. He was taunting her now.

"No guards. I'll come to you, but only as a lover or not at all," she told him, refusing to back down.

"Why?"

"As lovers, we'll be equals. Otherwise, I'll just be another task on your list of responsibilities."

He didn't take advantage of her speech to invade her mouth. "Your blasted independence," he muttered. "You refuse to see the danger." He dropped his hands, and the cold rushed in where his hands had rested.

She shivered. "I think you're wrong. There's no danger. I wonder at your motives for insisting there is."

Her taunt hit home. His eyes darkened as they swept over her face, pausing on her mouth, then her throat, before glancing at her breasts. He looked away.

"You can make me want you," she admitted as if he'd spoken. "You can make me weak with longing. But I'm still my own person. Neither love nor passion can change that."

He sighed and pulled her hands from him. "All right. You win. I'll leave you to your own devices."

She couldn't believe he'd given in. "I don't want your guards lurking around, following me," she warned, "or I'll call the police and have them arrested."

His grip tightened on her wrists, then he let her go. "I think you really would."

"Believe it."

"Okay. I get the message. I'll tell my security chief to call off the guards tomorrow." He stepped back from her. "Do you have anything to eat? I'm hungry after all that rowing."

It took a few seconds for her brain to process the request. Sutter was as unpredictable as a sea-driven storm. "Grilled cheese sandwiches?" she suggested. He nodded.

They went into the kitchen. He raided the refrigerator for his favorite kosher dill pickles while she melted butter into a skillet. When the food was ready, they sat across from each other at the table.

It was like old times, but those days were gone forever. Sutter was going to have to accept that. She wanted something different from him. Maybe he was leery of love, but she wasn't.

Meredith locked the lab door, checked it, then started down the steps. Thank God it was Friday. She couldn't have borne another day indoors. August was a miserable month in the central valley. The university wanted to shut down the building during the long break until fall term, so she was going to have to take the rest of the month off, it seemed. She'd use the time at her place to work on the data from her findings.

At her house, she found a message from a married friend on her answering machine telling Meredith that she was at the pool. Meredith changed and went down. She tossed her towel on the chair beside the friend, said hi, then swam laps in the pool. It was too hot for any other kind of exercise. After twenty minutes, she turned on her back and kicked lazily from one end to the other until her heartbeat dropped to normal, then she got out.

She rubbed her hair with her towel, then wrapped it around her body sarong-fashion. "How's it going?" she asked Sandy, who'd married and moved into the complex before Meredith had decided to move there. Sandy was a teacher. Her husband was a doctoral student like Meredith.

"Okay. Summer school is out, so I'm free for the rest of the month." She pinned her hair more securely on her head. "A cool spell is supposed to be here tomorrow. I'll believe it when I see it."

Meredith laughed. "I think they mean ninety-five instead of a hundred and five."

"I'll melt!" She fanned herself with a paperback book. "How's the work going?"

"Fine. We're taking the rest of August off, too. It's just too hot to stay in the lab, and the other grad students want to go home for a while. One of them lives in the mountains of Montana. I'm thinking of asking if I can go with him."

"I don't blame you." She looked at her watch. "It must be time to fix supper. We're tired of salads, but I refuse to turn on the stove."

"Tuna salad is a staple at my house," Meredith confessed.

They laughed, talked a few minutes more and said goodbye. Meredith slipped into her clogs and returned to her flat. A man sat on the steps.

She halted, startled, then went forward with a puzzled smile on her face. "Terry?"

The young man from the marina stood. "Hey," he said, "I was in the neighborhood and decided to take a chance on stopping. Does dinner out appeal to you?"

She laughed. "Does it ever! Come in and let me change into some clothes."

"I like what you're wearing."

She smiled at him without picking up on the compliment. After opening the door, she motioned him in. "There's tea in the fridge. Help yourself. I'll only be a moment."

She showered and changed into a skirt and matching top printed with large blue flowers. A blue silk flower went behind one ear after she fastened her hair back on one side. A dusting of powder and pink lip gloss, and she was ready.

When she rejoined Terry, he was standing in front of her rainy-street picture. He turned and whistled.

"Thank you, sir." She picked up her purse and took his arm. "Tell me how T.C. is doing. Is he still cadging snacks off every boat that pulls into the marina?"

"Yes. He leads a charmed life."

"What happens to him in the winter?"

Terry shrugged as they left and walked toward his car. "He only showed up in late February."

"Oh."

They went to a nearby seafood house. Meredith enjoyed hearing about the people who stayed at the marina. She found Terry was much more entertaining than she'd remembered. She hadn't given him a fair chance against Sutter.

Pulling her thoughts away from that direction, she laughed at a story about one of her father's fishing buddies and was surprised to learn that her father and Genna had rented a boat and gone fishing one day last week.

"Seems to be a romance developing there," Terry said. His eyes were warm as he gazed at her.

"I hope so. That's what I planned when I schemed to get them together," she admitted, "but you never know how things are going to turn out."

"No, you don't." He glanced at her when the waiter came over with the dessert tray. "How about ice-cream pie?" he asked. "That sounds good to me."

"Can we share?"

"Sure."

Over coffee, Meredith realized she really was having a good time. In fact, she was more relaxed than she'd been all summer. This was what she needed—someone who was fun and made no demands, who looked at her with interest but without those blazing flickers of hunger that sent the flames shooting through her.

"So, how are things with your friend?" Terry asked.

"Genna?"

"Sutter, I think his name was."

Terry looked directly at her, and she realized he was asking about her relationship with Sutter. "I've not seen him for a month. I suppose he's busy with his company."

"Hmm." Terry's smile showed obvious relief.

Darn Sutter, she mused. He scared off other men with just a glance. If he ever went after a woman...

She lifted her cup and took a sip of coffee. The clock, which was mounted on a piece of burl wood with a sailing ship painted on it, indicated the time was almost eleven. She was surprised. "I had no idea it was getting so late. You have a long drive back and an early day tomorrow."

"Why don't you come out and visit with me and T.C.?" Terry asked. "We could use the company. It's slow now. All the boats are rented this week."

A smile lighted her face. "That's a wonderful idea. We could have a picnic on the pier."

They made their plans on the way back to her apartment. There, Terry kissed her good-night, the kiss brief and chaste. He was a nice person, not pushy like some men she could, but wouldn't, name.

Meredith sat on the dock, her feet dangling in the cooling waters of the river. T.C. lounged beside her, his body stretched out along her thigh.

"It's really too warm for this much togetherness," she scolded, rubbing his black ears. He merely purred louder.

Actually, the heat had broken, and the temperature was a balmy eight-three. She and Terry had eaten a picnic lunch outside, then he'd taken her on a boat ride along the delta.

She'd spoken to her father's fishing friends who spent the summers on their houseboat. All in all it had been a pleasant way to spend the first day of a new month.

She looked at her watch and saw that it was after seven. Most of the rush-hour traffic would have cleared out by the time she reached the city. She patted T.C., then ambled back to the marina office. Terry was on the phone. She waited outside for him.

When he appeared, she held out her hand. "Thanks for a lovely day. I've really enjoyed it."

"I have Friday night off. How about a movie?"

"Umm, could you call me? My father is supposed to come over, and I'm not sure what our plans are."

"Sure thing." Terry took her hand and pulled her closer. He settled his hands lightly on her shoulders and kissed her. When he raised his head, he sighed. "No lightning bolts, huh?"

She was apologetic. "Well, not yet."

He squeezed her lightly and let her go. "Tell you what. Call me when you feel like seeing someone. I'll come running anytime I'm free."

"Thanks." She was touched by his willingness to wait for her.

He walked her to her car and opened the door. A meow stopped Meredith from starting the engine when she was buckled in. T.C. ran to the door and jumped inside as if determined not to let her leave him behind again.

"Well, I'll be damned," Terry said.

She frowned. "Do you think he'll stay with me? He'll have to be a house cat. I'd be afraid he'd get run over in town."

"He seems happy enough."

The cat had taken the passenger seat and was busily washing himself. He gave her a questioning glance. She started up, but left the door open so he could get out if he was afraid. He leaned his front paws on the dash and peered out.

"Okay," she said with a laugh. "Here we go."

She and Terry waved goodbye, then she rolled up her window and took off. T.C. watched the scenery, moving from window to window the whole trip. At her apartment complex, she scooped him securely into her arms, her hand firmly clasping his front paws so he wouldn't scratch her if he became frightened.

She stopped when she came to her sidewalk. A man was seated on the front steps. "Easy now," she said when T.C. tensed.

Sutter stood when he looked up and saw her coming toward him. He didn't smile, nor did he comment on her armful of cat. He simply lifted the animal from her and handed her a note.

She read the brief message: "You don't fool me with the blonde. I know your woman has dark hair. Like mine did."

Jealousy skewered her heart and roasted it over hot coals. "You've been seeing a blonde?"

He gestured impatiently. "I took my secretary out to lunch for her birthday last week. He must have seen us."

He shoved the note back in his pocket, then followed her inside when she opened the door. He put the cat down after he closed the door behind them. T.C. sniffed cautiously.

"The note was delivered at one," Sutter said. "I've been trying to call you all afternoon. At five, I decided to come here and wait."

"I went to the marina."

"So I see." He took her hand and urged her to her bedroom. "Get your bags packed. You're coming home with me."

"Sutter—"

"No arguing. You've got your proof. It's too dangerous for you to live alone."

She looked at him for a long minute. There was a restless tension about him that she'd not seen before. Too much coffee and too much work, she decided. He looked so tired, she hated to argue, but she had her needs, too. "I'll go home with you on two conditions."

His face looked like chiseled stone. "Name them."

"One: T.C. comes with me."

"Agreed. The other?" He was all business.

"My birthday present. The one I asked for."

The silence was like a sudden frost, a cold hard crystal of desire and denial. She was caught in the crosswind of his will against hers, but she didn't flinch.

There is a tide in the affairs of men... And women, she thought. This was hers. By being with Sutter, living with him day after day, she'd show him that together a man and woman could build a wonderful life, one that he need have no fears about lasting.

She experienced a growing urgency inside and paused to test her instincts. Yes, this felt right. Like the swelling of a bud on the vine, she knew they were both ready for this.

She loved him. She thought he loved her. Now if she could convince him to take a chance on that love...

Chapter Nine

Sutter dropped his hand to his side. Not a flicker of emotion appeared on his face. He gestured toward the cat. "He has to go to the vet for a checkup and shots. He'll have to be altered."

"I know." Meredith scooped up the young tomcat and carried him into the kitchen. She filled a cereal bowl with water and put it and T.C. on the floor.

The cat hunkered down and drank, his tail twitching, his eyes and ears alert to danger in this new place.

She smoothed his black fur and sympathized with his fear. She knew the feeling. "And the other?"

"We'll talk about it."

"When?"

"Don't push." He started toward her bedroom. "Let's get you packed and out of here."

"Tonight?" Her voice vibrated with emotion. She wasn't sure if she was asking about leaving or loving. She looked at his hands and remembered how they'd felt on her skin that night on the boat. His touch had been wild on her, and so sweet and gentle it could bring tears to her eyes. She wanted it that way again.

"You're going home with me tonight, yes," was all he said.

"I have to stop at the store for some cat food and litter."

"I know."

He was all business after that. He retrieved her luggage from the top of the closet and opened the cases on the bed. When he saw that she'd started on the task, he left the room. She heard him talking on the kitchen phone a minute later.

She filled her small case with underwear, pajamas, swimsuits and slippers. Into the large one went casual summer slacks and tops, shorts, T-shirts and sandals. It was only half-full.

Standing in the middle of the bedroom, she thought of the night still ahead. Tremors ran along her nerves. Her bed, virginal and pristine with its white bedspread scattered with flowers, seemed to mock her excitement. *Tonight.*

She rushed to her dresser, removed a nightgown and robe of sheer pink lace, and tucked them beneath her underwear.

Sutter returned. He scanned her clothes, then went to the closet. He selected several dressy outfits including a black cocktail dress that she'd bought on sale but hadn't worn. He tossed in a pair of black high-heeled sandals.

"What are those for?" she asked.

"We'll have some social engagements to attend. There's a cocktail party Friday night at the home of a client." He smiled for the first time. "We got the new contract."

"The one you and Dad were working on while we were on the delta?" At his nod, she threw her arms around him the way she would have long ago. "That's wonderful!"

His arms swept round her, crushing her in his embrace. When she leaned back to look at him, his mouth moved onto hers, taking her with a fierce hunger that assuaged her earlier doubts. She'd been afraid he didn't want her.

The hard pounding of his heart assured her he did. His hands slid down her spine and cupped her buttocks, bringing her into full contact with his body. Yes, he wanted her.

He opened his stance, and their bodies flowed together in an instinctive molding, male to female. He moved against her, his arousal burning into her, sending sparks through her. She clutched a handful of his shirt, moaning as need rushed anew from some hidden chasm inside her.

One large hand slipped farther along her buttock and cupped the brazen hotness between her legs. He caressed the skin next to her shorts and found the edge of elastic that protected her from the final contact. A shudder ran over him as he paused near the threshold of her desire.

"Meredith," he groaned. She'd never heard his voice so husky and strained. He released her. "Let's go."

Weakness gripped her. She could hardly stand. *Tonight*.

They closed the suitcases, and he carried them while she gathered her purse and the cat, who was walking along the back of the sofa, obviously feeling more at home.

"Poor darling," she murmured. "All this moving around. You may wish you'd never left the marina before the day is over."

Sutter settled her in his car, T.C. in her lap. The tomcat gave her a questioning meow. She rubbed his sleek fur.

After storing her luggage, Sutter climbed in beside her and drove off.

They stopped at a store near his town house. While she selected food and a bowl, cat litter and a litter box, Sutter went off on a quest of his own. He met her at the register and laid his purchase next to hers.

"I'll get it," he said, taking out his wallet.

She didn't argue. Feeling like the original scarlet woman, she fled to the car. Sutter rejoined her, and they continued on their journey.

He gave her an amused glance. "Are you on the pill?"

How could he be so cool about it! She shook her head.

"What kind of lover would I be if I didn't take care of my partner?" he demanded, stopping at a red light. He ran a finger down her cheek. His touch was cool on her heated skin.

She laughed, only it came out more like a shaky sigh. "It's just that I've never...I mean...I suppose a person has to get used to certain things."

"If we're going to be lovers," he agreed, "you'll have to get used to a lot of things."

She recovered her poise. "Such as?"

"Falling asleep in my arms. Waking in the morning to the feel of my lips on you...all over you. Every inch of you."

His words set fires inside her, making her hot all over. She had to be glowing like a blast furnace.

The light changed and he concentrated on driving once more. But he went on telling her what to expect.

"We'll make love at night, and in the morning when we wake up. At noon, perhaps."

She choked at the images that rose in her mind.

"In my office. You'll have to go there with me every day," he informed her. "I'll put you on the payroll. You may as well earn your keep. You can work with your father.''

She held up her hands. "Stop. You're moving too fast."

He pushed a button and his garage door opened. He pulled in, killed the engine and turned to face her. His smile was sardonic. "You might not think it's fast enough."

She said nothing, but she was troubled. She'd thought he would admit her to that secret walled-off place inside him, but she felt he'd withdrawn even further.

He retrieved her bags, leaving her to ponder his words. She picked up T.C. and the grocery bag and followed him through a door that opened into the kitchen. She placed the bag on the counter and released the cat, who began to sniff out his new quarters. He gave her a patient cat look.

She prepared a bowl of food and the box of kitty litter. After tossing Sutter's purchase to him, she folded the bag neatly and stored it under the sink. T.C. purred against her legs.

Sutter placed the bowl on the floor under a built-in desk. The litter box went into a convenient laundry room close by. He placed his package in his pocket.

"Your room is this way," he said.

He led her up the stairs. Open doors revealed a large master suite to the left, a reading nook straight ahead, and another suite, complete with sitting area and private bath, to the right.

She grimaced at the gray carpet that had been used throughout the town house. The walls were oyster white. Get rid of the border with the burgundy print, she thought. Perhaps some splashes of red or primary yellow to brighten the place up...

"Are you hungry?" he asked, putting her luggage on the bed.

"No."

"I'll see you downstairs." He left her.

Hands trembling, she unpacked as quickly as possible. Would he come to her in this bed, or would he take her to his? The protocol of lovers was entirely foreign to her. She'd have to let him guide her through the first awkward moments. *Tonight.*

Frowning, she debated changing to her nightgown now or later. Now, she decided. She stripped and headed for the shower. Ten minutes later, she blew her hair dry, powdered and perfumed her body as if she were a priestess preparing for a secret, profound ritual, and donned the pink lace gown and robe.

She gazed anxiously at herself in the mirror. Her cheeks flew bright flags of excitement. Her lips were already rosy. She was ready. After slipping on pink fuzzy scuffs, she descended the stairs, her heart beating harder with each step.

Sutter stood in the dark living room, his gaze on the city lights spread like a magic carpet below them. He didn't turn when she stopped beside him.

"When I was a kid—we were poor, my mother and I— I used to dream of a place like this when I delivered papers in a similar neighborhood." He sounded so strange, almost sad.

"And now you're here," she said. She slipped her cold hand into his, needing the reassurance of his touch. She fought an impulse to grab him and hold on as tightly as she could. He seemed terribly far from her on this night that was to bring them together as they'd never been before.

He looked at her then. For a second, she saw the leap of raw passion in his eyes—a primitive hunger, hope, pain, that shredded her fears and left her open to him and him to her. It was gone in an instant.

A slow smile lit his face. "Let me look at you." He did so, leisurely, thoroughly. "Very pretty." He brought her hand up to his mouth and kissed each knuckle.

Alarm ricocheted through her chest, bouncing off her heart in a rapid fire of warning. Something wasn't right.

"Sutter, what is it?"

He questioned her with a glance. "Isn't this what you want? Us alone, on the way to becoming lovers?"

She gestured helplessly. "Yes, but..." Knowledge tore at her heart. "You don't want it."

"I want you." He laid her hand on his chest so she could feel his heart thumping against her palm. "I've wanted you for years. Is that what you want to hear?"

"No." She moved reluctantly from him and sat in a black leather chair. "I'm not sure," she added. She managed a tight smile. "I guess I thought there'd be more... intensity." This wasn't going well at all.

Sutter opened a cabinet and poured two glasses of wine. He gave her one, then sat opposite her across the glass-and-black-lacquer coffee table.

"You'll have to tell me what you expect from your lover."

Your love. A renewal of the passion we've shared, filled with all the wild, sweet yearning and without this cool calculation as if you have a job to do and you aim to please your client.

"Perhaps... more passion," she suggested. She sipped the wine, staring at him over the glass, watching his reaction.

"I assure you I'm on fire for you."

She sat the glass down and leaped to her feet. "Not like this. You're ruining it. On purpose." She held his dispassionate gaze for a few seconds before despair clogged her throat. She turned and ran, afraid she'd cry in front of him.

An arm closed around her waist just as she reached the first step. He spun her around. "Like this?" he demanded. His gaze was no longer cool and distant. It burned over her.

Their lips were on the same level. He kissed her with a savage passion that was no less intense for being controlled. He let her see his raw hunger but not the rest of his passion, not the part he kept locked away deep inside, the part she wanted to reach.

His fingers thrust into her hair, cupping her head, holding her captive to his ravishment. After a stunned second, her body responded as it always did, warming, opening.

He pushed inside her mouth, taking her by force, but she was ready now. She answered him, turning his desire back on him, arching her body against him, pitting her needs against his.

Finally he tore his mouth from hers. "I want you," he said. "I want you like hell. I want you deep and hard and as fast as I can possibly take you."

"Sutter!"

"I don't want to be gentle. I don't want to consider your maidenly inhibitions—"

"I haven't any."

"Like hell," he muttered. "You stampeded out of that store like a fox running from the dogs when I walked up to the checkout counter. If you'd been any redder in the face, you'd have stopped traffic dead still."

"All right, so I'm a little inhibited," she retorted, feeling her face grow warm again.

He gave a snort of laughter and caressed her cheek. The tenderness was back in his eyes. He'd often looked at her with tenderness. She wanted the passion.

"Do you always talk your way through a love affair?" she demanded. "How ever does a person stay in the mood?"

"You'll stay in the mood," he assured her. "When I'm ready to take you on that particular journey."

"You're not ready tonight?" Her gaze dropped to his waist and below. He was still ready.

"You're not," he corrected. "The timing isn't right. Go on to bed, Meredith. It's late, and we have to work tomorrow."

Confused by this change, she let him point her upstairs. She went to her room and closed the door. A black streak slipped past her just in time. T.C. jumped onto the bed, sniffed the pillows and decided on the side he wanted.

"Am I going to be stuck with you for a bedmate forever?" she asked, taking off the robe and tossing it over a chair. She felt tense all over as she slipped beneath the sheet.

With a sharp and sudden cry of disappointment, she realized Sutter would never come to her. Not tonight, not tomorrow night, not ever. With every word, even though he'd been telling her how much he wanted her, he'd built the wall around his heart higher. He'd used his passion to try and frighten her away. When that hadn't worked, he'd shut himself off behind his iron control.

What happened, Sutter? Did I get too close tonight? Are you afraid making love will crack your fortress?

Meredith awoke to the feel of paws kneading her midsection. "It must be time to get up," she mumbled, her throat sore from the tears she'd refused to let fall during the night. She pushed T.C. off and let him out the door before heading for the shower.

With the warm water pelting over her body, she considered her emotional state and decided on her reactions for the day. With Sutter, she'd better be prepared for anything—hot anger, icy reserve—anything! However he acted, she would be calm.

As if to dispute her decision, her heart pounded with an increased rhythm. All night she'd fought a wild yearning. All night she'd resisted the temptation to go to him. All night she'd wrestled with uncertainty.

What if she'd gone to him? What if he'd sent her away? What if he'd accepted her, and they'd made love? Would he have regretted it this morning? She sighed. There was no way to know.

The warmth of the water induced an image of his hands running over her, hot and tireless in his desire for her. She knew, on some deeply instinctive level, what his body would feel like against hers—hard and strong, throbbing with passion, yet gentle, caring. Dear God, how sweet it would be!

She gritted her teeth and got on with her task. Soon she stood in front of the mirror in the bedroom. Behold, the new woman, she coached her image as she dressed. She'd be tougher, more modern in her outlook on life and love, the sophisticated woman of the new age.

Later she strode into the kitchen wearing a peach sundress with a short jacket. The color added a rosy hue to her complexion, which needed all the help she could give it. She felt pale and washed-out after all the mental battles.

Sutter sat at the table, reading the paper. T.C. crunched on his food beneath the built-in planning area.

"Good morning," she said, injecting a bright note into the greeting. What if she went over and kissed him...

Sutter looked up, his gaze taking in everything from the way she'd pulled her hair to one side with a comb to the white pumps on her feet. A shower of tingles radiated warmth along her nerves.

Looking at him more closely, she noted the shadows in his eyes and the lines of strain on his face. He didn't look as if he'd slept any better than she had. Good. Why should she be the only miserable person in the house?

Guilt washed over her at the uncharitable thought. So much for the newer, harder woman.

"Good morning." He rose. "I'll get your breakfast."

An elemental stubbornness crackled through her. She wasn't some languishing maiden who had to be treated delicately in the face of disappointment. "I can fix my own."

"It's fixed," he snapped.

She laid her research notes on the table and let him serve her a breakfast of bacon and pancakes, complete with orange juice and low-fat milk. "Very good," she complimented when she finished.

"It came from your place."

She glanced at him in surprise.

"I cleared out your refrigerator while you packed." He returned her stare, a challenge in his eyes.

Aching for a fight this morning, was he? Well, he wasn't going to get one from her. She'd be so nice she'd drive him crazy before the week was out. Then he'd let her return to her home.

"I need to type up my notes. I thought I'd do that today. I also need to update my résumé and forward it to the National Park Office for a river study job with them. I'll put you down as a character reference, since you know me so well."

Sutter ignored her taunt. "There's a computer in your father's office you can use."

"Thanks," she said. "What time do you go to work?"

"Whenever I feel like it."

"Right. You're the boss."

A smile broke over his face. "Remember that and we'll get along like a house afire."

"Really?" She contemplated him through narrowed eyes.

Sutter didn't answer. He put the dishes into the dishwasher and closed the cat in the utility room. "Until he gets the hang of things around here," he told her.

She ran upstairs, brushed her teeth, put on makeup and was ready to leave when Sutter called to her. The garage door was open and the car running when she dashed down to join him a minute later. She climbed in and they were off.

Traffic rushed along at its usual Friday pace, the commuters anxious to get to the office and claim their paychecks. One more week, a few more dollars.

A blue Mercedes stopped beside them at a light, its horn tooting a friendly hello. Meredith instantly recognized the driver... the interior designer who'd done Sutter's headquarters and his town house. Red-hot jealousy grabbed her heart like a pit bull and wouldn't let go.

The woman smiled at Sutter in a private, smarmy manner that issued an open invitation before she gave Meredith a cold glance from her dark eyes. Sutter waved at her and smiled back, then glanced at Meredith.

She probed his gaze, wondering if he'd been lovers with the smartly attractive businesswoman. Meredith couldn't picture it. The woman was too hard-edged; the black hair was too sleek, the makeup too perfect for her to ever indulge in passion.

"She's cold," Meredith said in a cool tone.

He raised one dark, challenging eyebrow. "You don't usually disparage people you don't know."

"I don't need to know her. Her smile drips ice."

"I thought it was warm."

The light changed to green, and he shoved the pedal down. The car surged forward, beating the other vehicles by half a length. The Mercedes lost its place to a car that wanted in front of it.

Meredith was secretly pleased. "For men, not for women," she explained. "She's the type who doesn't have woman friends."

He flicked her an irritated glance. "You've become quite the psychologist of late, haven't you?"

She laughed, a version of the new, tougher image she'd adopted. "I don't have to be a psychologist to read her."

"Or me?"

"No, you're a closed book," she replied seriously. "Things are changing between us, coming to a head, so to speak."

"So it's war," he murmured, one side of his mouth curving upward in a mocking half grin as if the outcome was already settled in his mind.

"A duel to the death."

He reached out and captured her hand. He brought it to his lips when he stopped at another light, and kissed the back, then the palm, causing her to catch her breath, then breathe rapidly. His gaze mocked her defiant words.

"Not to the death," he corrected. "Only until one of us gives up or gives in."

When he released her, she caressed his hard-planed cheek and drew one pink fingernail along his lower lip. He caught her finger between his teeth in a surprise move and sucked at the tip. Flames shot through her.

"It won't be me in either case," she said.

He pushed her hand away, his expression closed once more. "We'll see."

Determination bloomed in her. After all, she was living in his house and sleeping under his roof. Only his control kept them apart. He'd nearly made love to her before . . . two times.

"Oh, yes, my love," she murmured wickedly. "We shall certainly see."

Sutter, for once, looked startled.

The guard at the gate to CNI gave Sutter a pass for Meredith to wear clipped on her collar all day. Next Sutter took her to payroll where she related her social security number and was put on the CNI ledger as a consultant. Finally he guided her to an office on the second floor of the headquarters building.

"This is where you'll work," he said, opening the door.

"Doing what?"

"Whatever your father tells you."

Dr. Lawton looked up and smiled. "About time. When Sutter said you'd be working with me, I wondered whether to believe him."

Meredith couldn't believe her eyes, either. Her father hated driving in heavy traffic. "When did you get here? Did you drive over this morning?"

A flush rose in Richard's face. "I, um, decided to come on up last night after Sutter called and said you'd be staying at his place for a while."

She cast him a perplexed glance. "But where did you—"

"He's staying with Genna," Sutter broke in.

That explained a lot of things. With a relieved smile, Meredith went to the empty desk and put her purse in the bottom drawer. "Let's not waste time," she announced crisply. "I understand the boss is a tyrant."

Sutter snorted while Dr. Lawton laughed aloud. After Sutter left, Meredith turned to her father. "Well, shall we get started?"

He leaned back in his chair, tenderness in his eyes. "Don't you want to ask me anything?"

"About you and Genna? No."

"Your mother will always be the first woman in my heart," he said. "I think you know that."

Swallowing hard, Meredith nodded. "But that doesn't mean there can't be room for someone else, does it?"

"No," he said, his gaze thoughtful as he studied her. "Is this what you planned when you introduced us?"

"I'd hoped you two would like each other."

"And if we decide to marry?"

It took her a moment to identify the emotion that racked her heart. It was envy. But happiness glowed inside her, too. This was what she'd wanted for them. "I'd like that."

She met his gaze, his hazel eyes very like her own, and felt the bonds of their kinship reaching back into her childhood and beyond that to the love of a man and a woman for each other before she was even born.

"You were always a generous child," her father remarked in a husky voice.

She laughed in denial. "I have some notes to get in order, then I'll start on your stuff. What do you need done?"

"How about proofreading this report when you get time? I've gone over it for technical errors and made corrections."

They worked in silence the rest of the morning, each absorbed in the tasks at hand. When Sutter returned at noon, father and daughter were amazed that it was time for lunch. Sutter declared he was taking them out.

"Wow, lunch with the big boss," Meredith exclaimed with a false innocence. She fluttered her lashes. "Do consultants get the VIP treatment all the time?"

He gave her a sardonic grimace. "Only on your first day, so shut up and enjoy it."

"Yes, sir," she answered smartly.

"Someday..." Sutter didn't finish the threat, but an undercurrent of serious warning scorched the word.

She saw her father give her and Sutter a keen glance. With a start, she realized he was worried.

The stark possibility that she'd end up with a broken heart loomed before her. Maybe she wasn't as tough as she was acting.

Maybe not, but she'd take the risk, she decided. Win, lose, or draw.

Chapter Ten

Sutter noticed the message light on his desk telephone was lit up. He clicked the machine to rewind, then listened to the message that had been recorded.

"Hello, Meredith. This is Terry," a male voice began. "It's Friday, around five o'clock. Since I didn't hear from you during the day, I assume we're not on for tonight. I know I left it up to you, but I wanted to be sure. Call me by six if I'm supposed to come by. Otherwise I'm out of here."

Sutter's headache throbbed a bit more painfully. They already had plans for the evening, which Meredith had probably forgotten.

Annoyed, he wondered how Terry knew to call his home, then realized Meredith had forwarded her calls to his number. She might as well have broadcasted where she was staying. Anyone dialing her number and hearing his voice would figure it out in a second.

"Meredith!" he roared. He stalked out of his study, ran up the stairs and pounded on her door. "Meredith!"

"What?" she yelled.

He flung open the door. "Do you realize what you've—"

The sight that slammed into his brain brought him to a dead stop. Passion intermingled with fury, so blindingly hot, he almost melted at her feet. Only the fact that his body went perfectly rigid saved him from making a total fool of himself.

She stood next to the bed, one hand stretched toward the black dress lying across the cover. At that precise moment, she wore nothing but a black lace teddy...and looked exactly like the angel-devil that men dream about finding!

Sweat beaded his brow and upper lip. It collected on his chest and along his spine. "Sweet heaven," he groaned as another painful shaft of desire hit him.

She jerked the black dress in front of her, but the action hid nothing from his imagination, which was already going wild.

"Get out of here," she ordered.

He nearly laughed. She didn't realize he couldn't move.

Pivoting half-around, she flung the dress into the air and let it slide down her arms. She yanked it over her breasts and settled it into place around her hips. With her back still to him, she hooked the tiny fasteners at the front before facing him again.

"Enjoy the show?" she asked, turning to him.

"More than you'll ever know," he admitted.

Nature had given her perfect skin in shades of pink and cream. The hunger rampaged within, close to his breaking point. He knew how she'd be inside—like warm honey, hot and sweet and welcoming. He had only to reach out and take what he wanted…and give her what she wanted.

She's ready for a mate.

A different pain hit him, one derived from the knowledge that he wasn't the one for her. She needed a younger man, a softer one, he thought in a flash of keen insight. He stepped back, intent on leaving before he forgot his honorable intentions toward her.

"What were you yelling about?" she demanded, smoothing down the glossy strands of her hair. She looked calm, but the trembling of her fingers gave her away.

She'd tremble all over if I touched her.

He remembered his anger. "Did you have your calls forwarded to my house?"

"Yes."

He clenched his fists. "Don't you realize Fisher can call your house and be directed right to my place when he hears me answer instead of you?"

Her guilty look told him she hadn't thought of that. "I'll take it off." She went to the bedside telephone and dialed in the codes to remove the earlier command. "What was the message?"

It took him a second to remember. "Your friend Terry called. He said if he didn't hear from you by six, he'd assume your date was off."

"We didn't—" She stopped. "At least, I don't think…"

"You didn't have a confirmed date." Sutter refreshed her memory, jealous as hell and glad she'd forgotten. He glanced at the clock by her bed. Ten after six. Relief spiraled through him.

"That's right." Her brow smoothed out for a second before she frowned at him. "I still have to put my makeup on."

He nodded, retreated and closed the door. Going back to his den, he massaged his temple with one hand. It was going to be a cold day in Hades before he forgot this night.

When Meredith stood before Sutter thirty minutes later, she forced a cool composure to the surface while his gaze ran over her and lingered at the low neck of the dress. He looked as if he wanted to strangle her or devour her...and it didn't much matter to him which one he did.

A slow throbbing like voodoo drums began within her. She closed her mind to the sound, but no defense could withstand the heavy pulsating impression of his maleness. Wary, she skirted the issue of his masculinity and her attraction to it.

Warm fur purred against her ankles. She stooped and patted T.C. "I can't pick you up," she apologized. "This dress is silk, and I can't afford a snag in it."

"You look charming," Sutter said, his voice edged with a sharpness she associated with anger. "Are you ready?"

"Yes." It wasn't *her* fault he'd caught her undressed.

"We'll eat first. I have reservations—"

She laughed and picked up on his statement. "So do I. Something tells me I should be home. Alone."

His frown changed to cool amusement. "Feeling sassy tonight?"

"More like self-preserving."

"Remember that and you might survive till morning."

His dark taunt provided fodder for her churning mind on the trip to the restaurant. She didn't want to merely survive.

"I want to live," she told him without noting the fifteen-minute lapse in the conversation.

"Now you're showing some sense." He handed out the compliment while helping her out of his car. Inside the restaurant, their table awaited them, and they were seated at once.

"I meant I want more than survival. I want to live, really live," she continued.

"I know what you want," he said. His knuckles turned white on the menu, which he held up between them.

End of conversation.

Sighing, she looked over the selections. Frustration coiled in a tight ball in her stomach. Food didn't interest her at all. The old hunger manifested itself in a painful restlessness. Her heart beat wildly in her chest, skipping ahead, then slowing down.

At the end of dinner, Sutter signed the credit-card slip, and he and Meredith left for the party.

"That was a delicious meal. Thank you." Her voice came out low and husky, the sound intimate in the darkness of the car's interior. She cleared her throat.

He flicked her a glance, but didn't say anything. They arrived at a monstrous house in a rich neighborhood. A fountain shot plumes of water into the air in the center of the courtyard.

"They obviously never heard of the drought here," she said.

"It's recycled."

He kept his gaze on her for a few seconds, long enough for her to sense his hunger. A frisson ran down her neck and lodged in her throat, but she smiled, hoping she looked womanly and worldly, especially when the doorman opened the car door and held out a gloved hand to her.

She looped her hand over Sutter's arm when they went inside, not about to let him abandon her in a throng of celebrities. She recognized two TV anchormen and a movie star right off the bat.

"Impressive," she said, glancing around the huge entrance hall. Doors leading off to side rooms glittered with strappings of medieval brass. Straight ahead, in a ballroom with chandeliers that weighed more than she did, a mob of people mingled and talked.

Her heart dropped to her toes.

"Scared?" he taunted.

She stiffened her backbone. "No."

After meeting their host, Sutter guided her through the crowd. He knew several guests and stopped to speak, introducing her as a friend from his youth.

"Hardly," she protested. "I was the youth. He was an older man." She tossed him an arch glance, which drew laughter.

"Behave yourself," he warned when they walked on.

She moved in closer, letting her breast brush against his suit sleeve. The movement, meant to tantalize him, rebounded on her. She wanted to pursue the pleasure.

He faced her. "Don't start something you're not willing to finish," he ordered through clenched teeth.

Surprised, she realized he was nearer the breaking point than she'd thought. The fire that blazed from his eyes burned a hole right through her common sense.

"I won't," she promised, no longer smiling.

"Meredith?" a feminine voice called out of the crowd.

Meredith glanced around, then saw a young woman coming toward her, dressed in the most gorgeous gold lamé gown she'd ever seen. The dress clung to the blonde's skin and seemed a living, breathing part of her. "Susan," Meredith exclaimed, recognizing a school chum. "What are you doing here?"

"Visiting," Susan said. "This is my uncle's home. Who's this beautiful hunk with you?" She batted her lashes at Sutter. "Are you available, you handsome devil?"

Meredith managed to smile. "Sutter Kinnard. He's head of CNI. Watch him. He bites."

Susan sucked in a breath that swelled her breasts perilously over the top of the gold material. "Oh," she squealed in delight, "just the kind I adore." Laughing, she insinuated herself between them and led them off to join her group of friends.

After that Meredith rarely saw Sutter; at least, not without Susan hanging on to his arm and his every word. Her only pleasure rode on the fact that Sutter wasn't truly enjoying himself. He was attentive to Susan, but his heart wasn't in it.

"Care to join me in a dark corner? Would you let me kiss you on the neck? Would you let me take a little bite?"

Meredith smiled up at the handsome young man, who was probably twenty. "Sounds like you need a blood transfusion," she joked.

He grinned, exposing vampire teeth.

She recoiled, then laughed. "I haven't seen a set of those things in a hundred years." Vampire teeth had become the rage with the recent success of a TV series featuring a Draculean family.

"Ah, then you are one of us." He mimicked a Transylvania accent. He bent lower over her, then dipped down and pretended to bite her neck.

She pushed him away with a shudder of mock horror. He removed the fangs and took the chair next to her. "So, what are you doing for the rest of my life?"

"Going home," another male voice answered. Sutter held his hand out to Meredith. He looked the part of the *grand seigneur*. He only needed a sword to complete the impression.

"Oh, is it time?" She glanced at her watch. Close to midnight. My, how time did fly when one was bored. "What happened to Susan?"

"Ah, our fair Susan." Young Dracula spoke up. "She's probably looking for me. I'll go find her." He departed in a hurry.

Sutter looked in slightly better humor. "Shall we?"

Taking his arm, Meredith nodded and allowed Sutter to escort her out the door. "Somehow I think I might have fared better with the vampire than with you this evening," she remarked. "What's wrong?"

At the car, instead of opening the door, he pressed her back to it. "You," he growled. "You're what's wrong."

He ground his lips against her surprised mouth. She withstood the assault of his kiss for several seconds before her stillness registered on him. Against her body, she felt the unmistakable arousal in him. It spoke to the wild yearning that seethed just beneath the surface of her own control.

"Sutter, don't," she said when he lifted his mouth from hers. She wasn't sure of his mood.

"Why not?" he demanded. "You let that pup kiss you on the neck in front of a roomful of people. Why not me out here?"

"He didn't. He was just teasing. Oh, you're jealous," she murmured, catching on to his problem. "I see."

He withdrew immediately. "Get in," he said. He opened the door, and she climbed in. He drove home at a furious pace.

At the town house, she started straight for her room. Sutter was spoiling for an argument, and she wasn't up to it.

"Stay for coffee," he invited.

She paused midway on the steps. "No, thanks."

She looked down at him. He stood at the bottom, his hand on the banister, his lean fingers splayed out across the dark wood. As she stared into his eyes, the knowledge swept over her: it wasn't anger. It was more than that. There was a bleakness in him that spoke to her. And perhaps a restlessness that matched her own.

She shook her head, wondering if she should stay with him, and then she went on up to bed. She was in her pajamas when her door opened and T.C. dashed in. The door closed.

The cat leaped upon the bed, gave himself a desultory wash and settled on his pillow. Sighing, Meredith joined him.

They carried T.C. to the vet the next afternoon. Meredith held him in a towel so he couldn't scratch if he became frightened. After an examination and the necessary shots, the vet put him in a cage in the back. "You can pick him up tomorrow afternoon. We'll call you."

He smiled reassuringly at her anxious farewell. Sutter took her arm and led her outside. "It's a simple operation," he said.

"I know, but he's scared."

A reluctant smile curved his lips. "Yeah, well, I would be, too, if I were in his shoes." He looked at his watch. "We only have time to shower and dress before dinner."

They went to a formal dinner at the country club. Beside him at the table, she asked, "Do you think you can keep us occupied every night? Sooner or later, we'll have an evening at home. Then what will you do?"

"Eat you in one bite," he promised.

"I bite back," she warned, the sparkle of sensual excitement and challenge in her eyes. This week, she decided. If she didn't break through his defenses this week, she was going to give up and move far away, so far she'd never see him again.

It was ten o'clock when they returned to his home. "Coffee?" she asked, settling into a chair and kicking off her shoes.

Sutter cocked his head and perused her. "Last night you took off for your room as soon as we got home. Tonight you've decided to stay down here. Trouble making up your mind?"

"No. I know what I want."

"Do you?" Sutter almost growled with frustration. She'd flirted with him all night, her hand constantly settling on his arm as she made some point or other. She'd given him sidelong glances and secretive smiles. He was near the edge and he knew it.

She could drive him wild with a glance, a touch. Having her in the house was proving worse than he'd thought it would be. And he'd had no illusions about that.

"I want you," she said. She wet her lips.

It was the last straw. With a groan, he pulled her to her knees in the chair, until he could taste the honey of her lips. He probed and stroked and explored until his ears buzzed with the rush of blood through his head.

He sensed her yielding and knew he could take the embrace as far as he wanted. She held nothing back, but pressed her sweet body against him eagerly, making him ache for completion in her.

Sweeping his hands down her back, he cupped her hips and lifted her. He knelt on the floor in front of her and pushed between her accepting thighs. Her legs closed around him.

He realized he was shaking. Even his mouth trembled on hers, his need was so great. He wanted to take and take and take. . . .

A pain arced through him, and he tore his mouth from hers.

"Sutter," she protested, reaching for him again.

"Don't," he warned.

She stopped, puzzled, her eyes open now and dark with the passion he'd incited. Grief rocked through him. He was going to hurt her. God knew he didn't want to.

"It's no good, Meredith."

"Why?" she asked, her sweet voice trembling.

He pulled away from her arms and stalked out of the house. Meredith heard the snick of the dead bolt. He'd locked the door behind him so she'd be safe. Going to the window, she saw him stride down the dark street, his head low, his hands thrust into his pockets. Alone. The way he intended to stay.

What could she do? Sutter didn't want her love, he didn't trust it, but she needed to share it with him. She was filled to bursting and it was all for him, only him.

She went upstairs and put on her nightshirt. She didn't need a sexy gown to lure him. She'd use her love. It was all she had to melt the barrier of ice around his heart.

Sutter let himself into the silent house. The clock in his den struck two, reminding him he'd walked longer than he'd intended. He noted the lamp left on for him, its light welcoming him home.

Meredith's doing. Meredith, with all her sweet, giving ways, her bright sassiness that made him want to kiss her one minute and scold her the next. Mostly, he wanted to soak in her warmth, just melt into her....

All the fires of hell burned through him, searing his control, filling him with a wild desire only she could put out. God, if she only knew! Hours of walking couldn't cool him off.

He turned off the light and went up the dark stairs. At the landing, he paused and gazed at her door. If he went in, she'd open her arms to him. She'd take him into her, pour all her love over him, let him take what he needed.

He swallowed hard and stopped the train of thought. She believed in love. Maybe she knew what she was talking about. In her family, it seemed to have worked. But not in his. Love had never been enough to solve any problem in his life that he could remember. It only brought its own kind of suffering.

He closed his eyes and turned blindly toward his room. He'd not be the one to disillusion her. She had a glow that came from inside her, from some deep well of belief that he'd lost eons ago. He'd not be the one to douse that flame.

Opening his eyes, he faced the grim reality of existence. A momentary pleasure here and there, the challenge of work, the excitement of a deal and a new contract, that was life.

He stepped inside his bedroom and closed the door after him. His room was dark. It felt like a prison, but at least she was safe from him. For one more night.

Setting his thoughts aside, he went straight through to the shower, shucking his clothes in the dressing area on the way. Five minutes later, he stepped out, dried off and ran a towel roughly over his hair. He flipped out the light and headed for bed.

He found the covers already folded back, ready for him. That wasn't all he found. Feeling like one of the three bears, he stared at the dark mound curled in the middle of his bed. Unlike the bears, he knew immediately who it was.

Cursing under his breath, he switched on the bedside lamp.

Meredith looked at him, her eyes wide and luminous, the pupils dilated until they looked like black velvet. She smiled at him. "I thought you were never coming home."

Passion sucked him into a whirlwind of needs repressed far too long. He was at the edge. Hell, he was plunging right over.

"Get out." He gritted his teeth, his jaws so tight they nearly locked.

"No."

She stared at his body, and he couldn't stop the surge that had him raging like a stallion after a mare. Her eyes flicked back to his. Their radiance burned his conscience to a cinder.

Still looking at him, she rose to her knees and eased the nightshirt over her body, upward past her thighs and waist, past her breasts with their rosy nipples. His mouth went dry. He wanted to taste those delicate treats, to feel her writhe against him, giving and taking as much pleasure as they both could stand.

With a quick motion, she tossed the gown over her head and let it sail to the floor.

His breath left his body, and tenderness flowed in with the next quick intake of air. She was slender and small-boned, almost half his weight and strength, but she'd come to him without the slightest fear. He could see the trust in her eyes—a confidence in him and his control that he wasn't positive existed.

"Don't send me away." She smiled, but the telltale quiver of her lips spoke volumes. "I don't think I could stand it."

Pain sliced him into aching slivers. "I have to." He picked up her nightshirt and held it out to her. His hands were trembling as violently as hers. A shudder lunged through him.

She silently accepted her gown and pulled it back on. Looking as if he'd struck her a death blow, she climbed out of his bed.

"Meredith," he said, closing his eyes against the entreaty in hers, "I can't give you what you want."

He hated hurting her, but he was near the breaking point. She made him want to believe in love and all those fantasies associated with it—"Till death do us part" and all that stuff. But he knew better. He'd only hurt her worse if he let her stay, if they made love. Because she believed. And it cut him to pieces.

"What have I asked for?" she questioned, her voice as soft as a caress.

"Nothing. Everything."

He watched her, knowing the hunger was obvious, in his body and in his eyes, but he couldn't help that. To look at her was to want her. She went to the door and stood there for a minute, her head bowed as if she prayed, then she turned to him.

"I love you, you know," she said simply and walked out.

All that remained after she left was silence.

Chapter Eleven

The rattle of the Sunday paper alerted Meredith to Sutter's presence before she entered the kitchen. She hesitated before joining him, then she went in with a smile.

"Good morning," she said. Her voice came out warm, sultry even, and her smile became genuine when she saw the wariness on his face give way to surprise. "Did you think I was going to be a grouch this morning?"

"Truthfully, I didn't know what to expect," he admitted, his expression wary again.

"I've decided on a philosophical approach to our problems," she told him, deliberately taking a cheerful tone.

He gave her an oblique glance, then returned to the paper.

She went to the refrigerator and helped herself to orange juice. "Sooner or later," she continued as if he were eager to hear the rest, "it will all work out. Either love will win..."

A tremolo crept into her voice. She sipped the juice until she was in control once more.

"...Or I'll get over you and find someone else."

That brought his gaze back to her. She looked steadily at him, and this time, he turned away.

"Of course it'll be hard. I've loved you for so long. Since the moment I first met you. But if you don't love me..."

The telephone rang. Sutter pushed back his chair and strode out. He didn't look back.

She prepared a bowl of cereal and went to the table. It was several minutes before she could eat. Her hands were shaking.

"He'll probably want to take it easy for a few days," the vet advised. "If you have any problems, give me a call."

Sutter watched Meredith wrap the cat in a fluffy towel and hold him like a baby. The cat—a first-class con artist!—lapped up the attention as if he deserved it.

"Thank you very much." She smiled at the vet.

A curl of jealousy tightened inside Sutter. "Ready?"

She glanced at him and nodded. Still cuddling the cat, she followed him out to the car. He scanned the area quickly while he settled her inside and went around to the driver's door. He spotted Barney at the convenience market across the street.

The security guard flashed him a thumbs-up sign. Sutter let the tension drain from his muscles. He nodded before getting in the car and driving off.

The call he'd had from Ned Barker that morning had been a warning. Fisher was in the area. A definite identification had been made by the cop who'd been advising them on the case. Without an overt act by the troubled young man, there was still nothing the police could do.

Frustration seethed in Sutter. He wanted to pound Fisher with his fists until the guy vowed to clear out and leave Meredith alone forever. He rubbed his neck as the tension crept back in, making his muscles tight, preparing him for danger.

Violence. He'd hated it as a child. He hated it now—the barbaric cruelty of it, the reduction of a man to a savage—and yet, where Meredith was concerned, his feelings weren't civilized, he realized. Toward her, he felt…earthy, primitive…tenderness coupled with a fierce need to make love to her and an equal need to protect her. He wouldn't allow himself to hurt her. He'd kill any man who did.

Meredith laid a hand on his arm. "Is it me, or is something else bothering you?"

"It's just…" He couldn't tell her about the danger. He didn't want to scare her. "Nothing," he finished.

Guards were posted all around. Behind them, in an unmarked car, two security guards covered their tail. At his home, Barney and Ned cruised the neighborhood. They'd call him on the cellular phone if they saw anything suspicious.

The cat stirred and meowed, giving Meredith a pitiful look. "I know," she murmured. "You'll be uncomfortable for a few days, then you'll be good as new," she finished brightly.

"Huh," Sutter grunted.

The telephone jingled, causing her to jerk at the unexpected sound. So did Sutter. She watched him while he spoke tersely into the receiver.

"Yeah," he said. "Okay. No, I'll take her right in through the kitchen. No problem."

"What is it?" she asked.

"Nothing," he snapped.

She clamped her teeth together. His "nothing" sure had him tense as a caged cat. She studied him while he swung onto the street leading to his place. His glance swept over the pavement and along the sides. She was sure he could have described every car and person in sight.

At his drive, he hit the remote control for the garage door and slid smoothly inside and to a halt. She opened the door just as he pressed the control button again. With a grind of the chain directly overhead, the door started swinging down again.

T.C. tore out of her lap and leaped to the ground. Before the garage door closed, he sprinted outside.

"Oh, no," she cried, jumping out of the car with the towel clutched in her hand.

She pushed against the door just before it hit bottom, causing it to reverse with another grinding of the chain sprockets, and sprinted under it as soon as she could by bending low at the waist. She ignored a shout behind her.

"T.C.," she yelled, darting toward the street. She saw him duck under a parked car and ran up the sidewalk. "Here, kitty, kitty," she coaxed. She bent down at the car. "Come on, you silly thing," she scolded gently.

Reaching under the vehicle, she grabbed his collar and pulled him toward her. He let out a yowl of protest. She flipped the towel over his head and picked him up in it like a bundle of laundry. "There, gotcha," she exclaimed in triumph.

Another shout behind her brought her head up. She glanced at Sutter, who was running toward her, his expression furious. To her left, across the street, she saw a man with a gun.

Time dragged to a near halt. She saw Sutter gesturing toward her to get down. She dropped to her knees behind the car, cold hands clutching T.C., who'd gone strangely still. Briefly she spied Ned Barker, a revolver in his hand, the black hole at its end reminding her of an evil eye.

Sutter crouched beside her and pushed her head down when she tried to see what was happening. He crowded her against the car, his large body covering hers while he checked all around them. They seemed to stay that way for an eternity, his chest pressed to her back, his hands on her shoulders, forcibly holding her, grinding her knees against the grit on the pavement.

"You're hurting me," she said.

He eased his grip. She spoke in soothing tones to T.C., who wanted out of the suffocating towel. Poor thing, he'd probably lost at least two lives in the last two days.

"It's okay," a male voice called. The man ran to them and stooped, his gun on the top of the car.

"Barney!" Meredith smiled and tried to rise, but heavy hands prevented the action. "Sutter, for heaven's sake," she snapped. This cops-and-robbers play was wearing thin. "Let me up."

"It's safe," Barney assured them. "He's gone. We have a man on him. Maybe we can run him to ground. It'll be easier to keep him under surveillance if we know where he's staying."

Sutter rose and let Meredith up, but he kept her wedged between him and Barney. "Let's head for the house."

"This must be how a suspect feels," she quipped, walking along between the two men, each of them with a hand on her arm, their gaze moving from one spot to another in an endless search.

A shot rang out.

In an instant, a large body wrapped itself around her. Suddenly she was lifted off her feet. She hugged the cat with one hand and Sutter with the other as he ran, crouched low over her, into the garage. Barney guarded their backs, hitting the button to close the garage door just as another shot rang out.

Inside the apartment, Sutter put her down behind the sofa and pressed her to the floor. "Stay there," he ordered. He went into his den while Barney checked the windows.

Meredith's heart pounded. She released the towel, and T.C. scooted out and dashed for the stairs, his head low, his tail straight out behind him. He'd probably hide under her bed for a week. She didn't blame him.

The phone rang, causing every cell in her body to jump. She heard Sutter answer. Barney glided into the study. First Sutter, then the guard talked on the phone. After a minute, they laughed.

She stood when Sutter returned to the living room. Their eyes met and locked. A thread spun between them, invisible but growing, pulling them toward each other. She walked toward him.

He watched her impassively, then he stepped forward and met her, his arms closing around her as she reached for him, all the terror of the past few minutes catching up with her.

Barney came out of the study. "We think a truck backfired," he said with a sheepish grin. "That was the first 'shot.' One of our men got a little excited and fired into the air. Ned's going to read him the riot act, then he's going to skin him alive. We'll check the neighborhood out and post the usual guards. We lost Fisher several blocks from here, but I don't think he'll circle back."

"Thanks," Sutter said. "Tell Ned I'll talk to him tomorrow."

"Will do. I'll let myself out." He looked at Meredith, still held securely in Sutter's arms. "Don't take any wooden nickels," he said softly and left.

Meredith drew a shuddery breath and pressed her forehead to Sutter's chest. "I was afraid you'd be shot."

"Yeah, well, how the hell did you think I felt?" he demanded, taking her by the shoulders and holding her so he could glare down at her. "You little fool, you went running out without even looking to see who might be around."

The adrenaline pumped into her blood by the excitement turned into a fury that matched his own. "Don't call me names," she said irritably. Anger made her voice shake.

"I'll call you a lot worse if you ever do anything like that again, do you hear me?" His eyes blazed at her.

"Let me go! You've already bruised my shoulders and made me skin my knees—"

He released her with a curse and bent to examine her knees. Blood oozed from several shallow scratches and scrapes. "Come on, let's get you cleaned up."

He stood aside and indicated the stairs with a curt nod of his head. She went up. He took her arm and guided her into his room.

"Sit," he barked.

She slumped into an easy chair covered in burgundy velvet. As if a plug had been pulled, the tension drained out of her, leaving her incredibly tired.

She studied the room, refreshing her memory of it from her one other visit there. An abstract picture of gray and burgundy interwoven threads hung in the middle of one wall. The bed cover was a rich burgundy, quilted in squares of velvet and satin. The decorator had certainly been consistent in her color scheme.

Meredith tried not to think of Sutter and another woman in this room. She closed her eyes against the pain.

"Ouch," she said, jerking upright.

Sutter washed her knees. He dried them and rubbed on an antiseptic cream. "There, that should take care of any infection. The cuts aren't deep."

Meredith heard but didn't answer. She looked at his hand, resting on her thigh above her knee while he checked his handiwork. Her leg burned, but for a different reason this time. She reached out and smoothed the hair off his forehead, then let her hand linger in the thick strands.

He seemed not to notice. Instead, he stared at his hand on her leg as if contrasting the difference in their tans. Her skin looked golden against her white shorts and his darker coloring, she noticed. Slowly he looked up, his gaze running over her shorts, her pink shirt, her throat and face.

Her breasts became heavy and aching when he returned to them briefly. He looked past her, and she knew he was looking at the king-size bed that stood no more than six feet from them.

"Sutter," she said, anger transformed into longing.

He jerked his gaze back to her.

She ran her fingers through his hair and let them rest at the back of his head. She stroked his neck and watched hunger plunge his eyes into blackness as his pupils expanded with growing need.

"Don't, Meredith," he said, his voice harsh with strain.

"I want you." Desperation seized her, and she wanted to cry. He never wanted her, not enough to come to her.

He rose from his haunches. "Don't you think I know that? This isn't a good time—"

"It never is," she said, feeling the bitterness of his rejection grind into her soul. Fatigue returned. She wasn't up to an argument. She laughed, and it sounded so sad. "The time will never be right."

Sutter knew then that he couldn't leave her. Maybe it was vanity, maybe he was fooling himself because he wanted so badly to make love to her, but he knew he'd hurt her more by rejecting her than by taking her precious gift.

She was a woman, she was ready to be *his* woman, and he couldn't turn that down without wounding something deep and vital in her. "God knows I don't want to hurt you," he said hoarsely.

He took her hand and pulled her to her feet. She came to him, but without the usual glow in her eyes. She looked indifferent, as if she already knew how the embrace would end...just as it had so many times before when he'd kissed her.

But not this time.

He knew he wouldn't be able to stop this time. He knew it the way some wise people knew when a storm was coming or danger was near. The knowledge was in his bones.

Without hesitating, he unfastened her blouse...one button, then another, until he had them all undone. He pushed the pink cotton off her shoulders. The blouse fell and landed on the velvet chair. Stooping, he removed her sandals. And then her shorts.

Taking her hand, he guided her to the bed and stopped beside it. There, he kicked off his shoes, pulled off his shirt and peeled out of his jeans and socks. Now they were almost naked.

Her eyes were still dark.

"Glow for me, Meredith," he murmured. He threw the covers off the bed, stripped out of his last bit of clothing and removed hers. Gently, he lifted her and placed her in his bed.

The hunger grew in him, but it was all right. He didn't have to fight it anymore. He realized he couldn't. It was too great. He sat down on the bed. "Let me look at you."

The perfection of her body was a feast. Her shoulders sloped into the delicate curve of her arms, which rested on her thighs.

He traced the line from her neck to her wrist with one finger. He returned to touch her chin and sweep down her throat, his hand dark against the fairness of her skin. When he reached the dip between her breasts, he paused. Finally he chose the right one to explore first.

She drew a breath as if rising to his caress. He smiled as she let it out in a shaky sigh. His own fingers trembled when he plucked at the sweet puckered rose of her breast.

Pleasure bloomed and burst in him like some extravagant flower of nature. He bent to her, taking the plump nipple in his mouth and rubbing it with his tongue.

He heard her gasp, then her fingers raked into his hair, and she held him to her, coming to her knees and arching her back so that he could take all he wanted of her.

He thought he'd die from the pure bliss of it. The exotic flowers of passion bloomed and bloomed, filling him with their heady scent. He realized the perfume came from her, a natural blending of her unique savor and the cologne she wore.

She swayed, and he clasped her just above the waist. She seemed small compared to his breadth, yet she was solid and had a strength all her own that somehow matched his, at least in this.

For a moment, he went weak with need, then the strength flowed into him again, a flood of power that let him conquer the rampant desire of the moment and the harsh demands of his body.

When she made a little sound, he at once relaxed his grip. She impatiently pulled him tighter, then urged him to the side. They fell across the bed, still clasped together, and she smiled.

He looked into her eyes and forgot about his greater strength, the wildness of his desire. She could control him with a word, a glance, a touch.

I'll come to you as a lover or not at all. Yes, she wanted him like that . . . the way he wanted her!

He leaned over her, his thigh finding its own place between hers. She pressed against him, surprising him with her quick laugh, which ended in a throaty catch of her breath. He enjoyed her pleasure, his own increasing with each second, each pounding heartbeat of time. He kissed the delicate breasts that tempted him beyond thought.

With an urgent murmur, Meredith coaxed his lips from her breasts to her mouth. The kiss started hot and instantly became incandescent. She couldn't breathe. She found she didn't need to.

Waves of delight broke over her. She explored the tactile pleasures of touch with her mouth, her hands, her entire body.

While their lips and tongues and teeth discovered all there was or could ever be in a kiss, her hands roamed at will. She caressed his back and found the hard ridges of muscle on each side of his spine. By rubbing against him, legs against legs, pelvis against pelvis, chest against chest, she uncovered a wealth of sensation wherever skin met skin. His wiry body hair produced a wondrous abrasion against her smoother flesh.

She gasped as a new sensation, never before felt, joined all the others. He'd made a space between her legs and moved into it. Then he slowly rocked his hips against hers, and she felt his arousal at the threshold of her desire.

He lifted his head and looked into her eyes. "We can't stop."

She'd die if he did. She was so close...to knowledge...to life itself. Soon, she'd know all its secrets. Sutter would teach her all she needed to know.

He smiled slightly at her incoherent protest, and she knew he wouldn't disappoint her this time. For this moment, he belonged to her completely, and he'd not stop unless she requested it.

Heat enveloped her, spreading from that magical point of contact until it covered all of her.

"Yes," he breathed, "glow for me."

Again he moved, sliding his body against hers, and she felt the liquid warmth spread between them where they touched at that intimate place. He watched her, the tenderness in his eyes, but also the passion. This time, she'd have everything!

"Oh, Sutter, love me," she pleaded, "love me completely."

"I will," he promised, his voice a husky thread of sound.

He lowered himself to his elbows and gently attacked her neck with fierce kisses that had her writhing helplessly under him. She found the movement of her hips increased the pleasure, and she experimented with different rhythms until he groaned and told her to be still.

"Do you think I'm made of iron?" he asked.

She became very still, not sure what movements she was allowed to make. He chuckled, a strained sound against her ear.

"Do what you want," he said, sighing as if resigned to his fate. "I'll try to live through it."

With a tentative caress, she slid her hands along his spine until she could explore his hips, so lean and hard compared to her own shape. His skin there felt as smooth as her own.

She caught her breath as he performed the same actions on her, except he was bolder. He slipped a hand down the shallow cleft, where no one had touched her that she could ever recall, and found her exquisite softness and the hot moisture at the juncture of her thighs. She tried to press her legs closed, but his strong thighs blocked the movement. His fingers moved up and down.

"No, don't hold anything in," he coaxed when she bit at her lower lip to still the cry that rose in her.

Heat surged up her breasts and into her face. She closed her eyes helplessly. She'd been wrong. He did know her better than she knew herself, at least this part of her.

"Meredith."

She pressed her face into his shoulder to halt the rising passion and other feelings too mixed to sort through.

"Don't be embarrassed," he ordered, his lips pressing a rain of kisses over her temple. "This is wonderful and natural. Your body is reacting the way it's supposed to. It makes me want you more, feeling the way you respond, all hot and wet and welcoming."

He slipped a finger deeper into the space she knew was exactly as he described. There was no way she could hide her need for him.

Sutter felt her movement against his hand and experienced a burst of pleasure so strong, he had to fight the temptation to slide into her. It would take only one stroke....

But he didn't. For her, it had to be perfect. As good as he could make it. She was a virgin, and he wasn't sure...

"Come into me," she said.

"What?" He was so lost in his own task of pleasing her and trying to rein in his own pleasure, he wasn't sure he'd understood.

"I want you in me."

Desire exploded in a shower of fireworks, burning through his control. For a second, he wanted to plunge straight into the hot wonder of her. With an immense effort, he held back.

"I want to be there, dream girl, but not yet. There's more to this than what we've done so far. There're ways I want to touch you, hundreds of them, that will drive us both right out of our minds with pleasure—"

"You've already done that," she whispered, glancing at him, then closing her eyes again, quickly, as if, having opened everything else to him, she wanted to conceal this last bit of herself from him.

But it was too late to hide. He'd looked into her eyes and seen into her soul. She was giving him all that she was as a woman, as a person. She'd never learned half measures.

His hands trembled as he stroked her to higher pleasure, and for a moment, he felt unworthy of her gift. Then flames poured into him as she gasped and instinctively moved with the tempo that he set, and all thoughts submerged into the keen-edged pleasure of learning to please her.

Meredith pushed against the devastating ecstasy of his touch. He caressed her again and again, stealing her breath from her body as he took her higher and higher into pleasure's sphere.

She twisted against him, wanting more. And suddenly there was more. The stroking wasn't all on the outside, but had invaded her body. He ceased his careful movements, his wonderful enticement of her senses. She heard his breath catch and hold.

Slowly she pressed upward with her hips and realized he was poised at the threshold, ready to become a part of her. She squeezed her eyes shut, waiting for the final move.

ment. When it didn't come, she pushed impatiently against him.

"Meredith."

His voice held a warning, a groan of need that was fast going out of control. She exulted in the realization of power.

He moved away when she moved again, bringing an unconscious protest to her lips. She wanted all of him, not just this tiny tip that he was allowing. She thrust upward.

"Don't, baby," he gasped.

"Yes."

"I don't... want to hurt you."

She stroked her hands through his hair, loving him with all that was in her. "You won't. I want you now."

Opening her eyes, she stared into his, which were fathoms deep, his pupils expanded as if he looked far down into her soul. He probably did, for she could hide nothing now, not her happiness, not her passion, nor any part of her love.

Sutter knew he had to be careful. In her wild response, she'd obviously forgotten he wasn't covered. But he hadn't. He had to be the thinking one of this duet. He rested there, outside the paradise she offered, until he was sure of his control.

She moved unexpectedly, twisting her hips against him with a throaty sound of pleasure. He closed his eyes and held on for dear life, refusing to let them take that final step.

"Sutter," she murmured, her need urgent.

He resisted the natural urge to respond to her demand. He was ready for the final joining, only his willpower keeping them apart.

"You little devil," he admonished. "Don't you realize I could give you a baby if we finish this now?"

Her lashes flew open in surprise, then she laughed. He sucked in a deep breath, as he felt her laughter glide over him like a caress. No other woman could make him nearly fly apart just by laughing. Just by breathing. Just by *being*.

Meredith closed her eyes and tried to thrust her hips upward, but his weight held her immobile. Then he moved his hand between them and stroked her to the heights of passion again, until she squirmed in helpless abandon, and the pleasure grew and grew and grew, and again she couldn't breathe.

The feeling surged to new heights. Vaguely she was aware of his ragged breathing as he kissed her lips, her eyes, her lips again. His mouth ravaged hers, demanding entrance, then thrusting wildly in the same rhythm as his ceaseless caressing of her body.

Passion rose in her, a great conflagration of needs so strong, she couldn't have named them had she been able to speak. It burned through her like a rainbow—red-hot, white-hot, then blue, and she became incandescent.

"Sutter," she cried. "Oh, love, love."

After an eternity, she slid to earth, safe in his arms. She heard his voice, soothing and reassuring her.

"It's okay, love. You did fine," he whispered, pressing kisses along her brow. "You did just fine. You were wonderful."

She looked at him and couldn't look away.

The thread spun between them, silver and gold, as ethereal as a rainbow, as tough as the will to survive. It could still be broken, but it was there, tangible as a bubble.

"Don't leave," she said, feeling him withdraw.

"I have to."

She clung to him shamelessly.

He smiled and touched her lips, then ran a finger down the center of her chest. She was surprised to discover she was covered in a sheen of perspiration.

"Love's dew," he said, his smile infinitely tender, and licked the valley between her breasts. He moved and was gone.

A quick observation led her to say, "You still want me."

He nodded. "But first..."

"Oh," she said when he opened the bedside drawer and removed a packet. She watched the procedure with a great deal of interest that wasn't in the least maidenly.

"Now," he said, stretching his long, hard body over hers. Deftly he claimed his place, going straight down into the heated depths of her. "No problems?" he asked, his concern for her bringing tears to her eyes.

"None."

"You've always been athletic," he murmured, as if this fact explained something to him. He looked happy. With a wicked grin, he began a series of movements, his slow strokes bringing back the ecstasy as if she hadn't felt it moments ago.

She was embarrassed to let him see how much she wanted him so soon after he'd pleased her. He'd think her a selfish pig, a glutton for physical gratification.

Sutter was puzzled when she turned her head. Was she one of those women who, having gotten their pleasure, wanted the man to finish quickly and leave them alone?

"Do you want me to quit?" he asked, ready to do whatever she asked, taking nothing for himself. Just holding her and watching her ecstasy had been enough.

One look into her eyes, and he laughed, knowing the answer. Tenderness washed over him when a healthy blush spread over her face. She wanted him again!

"You've got to overcome these inhibitions," he teased "What's troubling you now?"

"You'll think I want only my pleasure, when you've had none," she explained against his shoulder.

"Ah, Meredith," he whispered. "I've been getting pleasure from the moment I touched you. Now...it's pure heaven, knowing you like what I've done."

She laughed and he felt the exquisite wonder of experiencing her laughter with his entire body.

"Like it?" she murmured provocatively. "Will you just shut up and do it all over again?"

"With pleasure, dream girl. With pleasure."

He did everything he'd done before and a little bit more. After all, she was an experienced woman this time.

Chapter Twelve

Meredith woke at dawn and found herself alone in the huge bed. Alarm shot through her, primitive and urgent. She flung the sheet aside and started to rise, then realized Sutter was probably having his breakfast.

For some reason, she thought it would have been easier to face him this morning—*the morning after*—in bed, rather than in the less personal parts of the house. If he'd kissed her awake, if they'd made love again, she'd have felt more...secure.

Fending off her trepidations, she went into his bathroom and showered. After toweling off and using his dryer to blow-dry her hair, she pulled on his discarded shirt and went down to the kitchen. The vinyl flooring was cold under her bare feet.

Coffee was in the pot, and she helped herself to a cup. Since Sutter wasn't at the breakfast table, she went in search of him.

She found him in his study, standing by the window and watching the pale gold crescent of the sun rise above the horizon. He wore a pair of blue tennis shorts and a T-shirt with the CNI logo printed across the back.

She must have made some noise, for he turned toward her when she paused inside the door. Despair tightened her throat as her eyes met his. He had apparently thought things over in the cool light of dawn and had decided last night was a mistake.

"If you apologize, I'll throw this coffee in your face," she warned, albeit with a smile.

His opaque gaze went straight to her heart. He'd closed himself completely off from her. He shoved one hand into his pocket and took a drink of coffee before answering. "How can I apologize for a taste of heaven?" he asked, matching her smile.

She could have cried. She didn't know what to expect between lovers, but surely there had to be more than this wary sidestepping like boxers sizing up their opponents.

"Why do I get the feeling we're back to square one?" She tilted her head and studied him, trying for a light touch. But tears kept melting her resolve. To her horror she realized they were going to **spill** over. She turned and headed for the kitchen.

"Meredith," he called.

"I'll fix some breakfast." She rushed for the kitchen, intent on getting away before she made a fool of herself. Closing the swinging door behind her, she set her coffee cup down and covered her face with her hands.

Nothing had changed. Why had she expected it?

Arms closed around her shoulders, and she was pulled to a warm chest and held there even though she struggled to get free. Her tears were dislodged and fell on his T-shirt.

"Let me go."

"Not on your life," he murmured. His arms tightened around her. He crowded her against the counter, his thighs opening to enclose her in his stance. "I'm sorry, Meredith."

She hated his apology. "Don't!" Laying a hand over his mouth, she managed a trembly smile. "I'm just not up on the protocol of lovers, or . . . or how to act the next morning."

"And I've ruined it for you, haven't I?"

His tone was gentle and so were his hands as they rubbed over her back, soothing and comforting her. She felt his chest rise in a deep breath, which he slowly released. Against her breasts, his heart thumped with a hard, steady beat.

With one finger, she traced the outline of his lips, recalling their wild, tumultuous paths over her body last night. Heat rose to her face. She'd responded just as wildly.

"No, you haven't ruined anything. Nothing can take away the wonder of last night. It was . . . I'll treasure it always."

He caught her hand and, closing his eyes, kissed the back and then the palm. "You make life **so** damned hard," he muttered.

"Why? I don't understand."

"You believe in fantasies." He sighed. "Perhaps it's better if I disillusion you than someone else. I'll try and let you down easy when the time comes."

"At the end of the year you promised me?"

"Do you think it'll last that long?"

His doubts hurt. So did the bleak unhappiness she saw in his eyes. And the worry. "It'll last all my life."

She felt his arms tighten around her. His head dipped to hers. "You almost make a believer out of me."

Almost. She closed out the pain. "Do you want food or . . . or sex first this morning?" she demanded, not quite as sanguine about it as she wanted to be. She wanted to show him she could handle their relationship without any hang-ups.

He blinked at the sudden change. His eyes darkened. He bent and swept her into his arms. "I want to make love to you," he said huskily. Then he carried her up the steps and to his bed.

"Put these calculations in and see what you come up with," Dr. Lawton requested. He handed Meredith a new set of figures.

She called up the spreadsheet and typed in the new numbers, her mind absorbed in the task. Facing her father and the world during the three days she and Sutter had been lovers hadn't been as difficult as she'd feared. Her private life was her own special joy or sorrow, to be shared or not, as she saw fit.

Sutter had been right in giving her a job. Writing her report and helping her father kept her mind centered on practical matters instead of spinning useless dreams.

One thing she'd decided on the way to CNI that morning: she wasn't going to hide her love from him. If he didn't like being reminded of her feelings, he'd just have to ignore them. Or try and talk her out of them if he thought he could.

The morning passed in a calming whir of activity. At eleven, she attended the regular Wednesday staff meeting with her father. He introduced her to the other engineers as his daughter and a whiz kid. "So don't try to impress her. She already knows computers."

Jim, the young man she'd met at the company picnic, didn't heed the advice. He sat next to her when they went to the company cafeteria and tried to hold her attention throughout the meal. She gave him an irritated glance when he once again interrupted her conversation with her father and one of the senior engineers on the new contract.

"Meredith."

All talk stopped as the big boss paused by their table. Meredith glanced up at Sutter. His face looked as hard as an ice sculpture. "Yes?" she inquired, her heart warming in spite of his ice-man approach.

"Could I see you in my office before you return to work?" He barely waited for her nod before departing.

She watched him leave, wishing he would look at her, oh, not as a lover, not in front of others, but with the warmth of simple gladness in his eyes. Or even friendship. She took a calming breath. She'd given up the friend for the lover.

"I'll take care of your tray," her father said.

He met her glance with a look of understanding. She wondered how much he guessed about her and Sutter's relationship. Whatever he thought, he kept it to himself. His only confessed worry was about Fisher's continued threats.

"Thanks," she murmured, grateful to get away from the annoying man on her left. She went upstairs to Sutter's office. His secretary was still at lunch, so she went to Sutter's door and knocked. "It's Meredith," she called.

"Come on in."

She'd hardly gotten the door open before she was hauled inside and the door slammed behind her. Sutter spun her into his arms and lowered his mouth to hers in a crushing kiss of impatient desire.

"Sutter," she gasped when he let her up for air.

"Was that guy bothering you at lunch?" he demanded.

"What guy?" She couldn't remember anyone.

Sutter gazed at her, his lush, black lashes half lowered over the slashing blue of his eyes. "Never mind," he muttered, his gaze on her mouth. He dipped his head and sampled her mouth with a dozen teasing kisses.

"Kiss me," she demanded, wanting more.

He lifted her and returned to his desk, settling in the large executive chair with a resigned sigh. He slid one hand along her leg and under her skirt. She stiffened and glanced at the door.

"No one would come in here uninvited," he said.

"What if it's an emergency?"

A grin kicked up one corner of his mouth. He rose, put her in the chair and locked both doors to his office. "Better?"

She matched his smile. He resumed their former positions.

"You look very pretty today," he murmured, nudging her blouse open with one deft hand. The ruffles of lace fell away to reveal an even more alluring camisole. "I've been seeing you in this since I watched you put it on this morning. And remembering that you wore no bra under it."

Pressing her back against the chair arm, he bent and kissed her taut nipple through the lace. When he raised his head, he'd left a damp spot on the cloth and had started the wild yearning to riot through her blood.

She glanced nervously at the door before she lost all ability to think.

"Relax," he advised in thickened tones. "My secretary won't be in for the rest of the afternoon. She's gone to the dentist."

"Oh."

Meredith decided to take his advice. She kicked off her sandals and lifted her legs over the arm of the chair. With a blatantly sexy glance, he slipped his hand along her stocking-clad leg until he reached his goal. She bit her lower lip as heat swirled through her.

"Trust me," he whispered, kissing her eyes closed.

"I do... with my life and with my body and with my heart."

"Meredith," he breathed next to her ear. Then he seized upon her mouth like a starving man, taking his fill while his hands played magic upon her body. He didn't let her go until she'd found total fulfillment in his wanton caresses.

Then he held her to his pounding heart while she rested in a mindless trance in his arms. At last she stirred.

"Are you...do you want..." She wasn't quite sure how to put the question into words.

He saved her the trouble. "Do I want you? Yes. Am I going to take you? No." He smiled lazily. "I have no way to protect you here."

She smoothed his tie between them. "You're always protecting me. From outside danger. From our passion. Why? How can you be so caring and yet deny that love exists?"

"I don't deny its existence." The coldness crept back into his eyes. "It's just that it doesn't work."

She sensed the chill came from a place deep inside him. "It can," she said, hoping her love would thaw his heart a little each day. She yawned, tired from their love play.

He pressed her head into his shoulder and shifted into a comfortable position. "Sleep. CNI can make it without our help for an hour or so." He closed his eyes.

Meredith and her father stood beside the floor-to-ceiling window, quietly enjoying each other's company and the lights of the city spread before them. He held a snifter of brandy while she sipped a liqueur from a tiny cut-crystal glass with a delicate stem.

From the kitchen, she heard a trill of feminine laughter and the deeper chuckle of a masculine tone as Sutter and Genna cleaned the dishes. Meredith had cooked an elegant dinner, which had turned out well. She smiled, pleased at the way things had gone.

In fact, she felt very domestic. Several times during the past week, she'd worried about that very thing. If she became too complacent, it would hurt even more when she left.

That time would inevitably come. Sutter's security force had discovered an old warehouse where Fisher was holed up, living the life of a panhandler during the day, hiding out at night. Sutter was thinking of offering the man a large sum of money to get out of town and not come back if Fisher didn't leave soon.

Maybe Sutter was tired of having her for a house guest. She reviewed the past two weeks. He didn't seem bored with her. He turned to her with a restless passion after dinner every night, and again in the morning. Twice at lunch, he'd called her into his office and locked the door against intrusion, giving her pleasure, taking none for himself.

She didn't understand. It was almost as if he were branding her as his own when he did that, but whenever she told him she loved him—which was often—the bleak cold settled in his eyes, and he'd be withdrawn for a while.

"Meredith?" Richard said.

She glanced at him with a questioning smile.

He put an arm around her shoulders. "I've asked Genna to marry me. Do you mind?"

She leaned her head back and stared up at him. "Mind? That's the most wonderful news I've heard in ages." A slightly worried frown crossed her brow. "What did she say?"

"She'd be honored."

Meredith let her breath out, not realizing she'd been holding it. "I'd hoped...when I introduced you...well, I thought it would be nice," she finished at his teasing grin.

"That's one reason we were a little hesitant," he confessed. "We wanted to be sure it was *our* attraction and not *your* enthusiasm that we felt."

"And you're sure now?"

"Absolutely."

"Well! When's the big day?" She set her glass down and clasped her hands excitedly between her breasts. "I hope you're going to have a big wedding, not one of those stingy affairs."

He threw back his head and laughed.

Genna preceded Sutter into the living room. "What's so funny?" she demanded. "Here Sutter and I were slaving away in the kitchen while you two stand here and crack jokes. Like father, like daughter," she told Sutter in confidential tones.

"I've told Meredith," Richard said, coming to Genna and slipping his arm around her waist.

"They're getting married," Meredith explained to Sutter. She searched his face anxiously for the coldness.

Sutter saw the plea in her eyes and wasn't sure what she was asking. Did she think he would cast a pall on the other couple's happiness? An unexpected lump tumbled into his throat and lodged there. He forced a smile on his lips.

"Couldn't happen to a nicer guy," he said heartily. "Keep him in line," he advised Genna with a wink.

"Meredith wants a big wedding," Richard told his fiancée.

Sutter's eyes jerked to Meredith involuntarily. She and Genna were hugging each other and going weepy the way women did at happy times. Sad times, too, come to think of it.

"I'll find a bottle of champagne," he said and hurried out to the kitchen. He removed a cold bottle from the refrigerator. He knew Meredith liked this particular brand and he had been saving it for some occasion. This one seemed appropriate.

Richard joined him. "Where are the glasses?"

"Up there." Sutter opened a cabinet.

While Richard placed fluted glasses on a tray, Sutter pried open the champagne cork. From the living room came the sounds of the two women talking, then laughing, and talking again. There was a special joy in hearing Meredith's laughter. A man could get used to it.

Suddenly he was hurting inside. He didn't understand why, and he resented it. Glancing at Richard and finding his old mentor gazing at him affectionately, Sutter experienced a jab of guilt. A man couldn't sleep with the daughter of a friend without feeling some pangs from his conscience, he supposed. Even in this day.

He wanted to explain that he cared for Meredith, that he hadn't taken advantage of her, that she understood he wasn't offering her fantasies about love and forever and all that.

"Ready?" he asked, his voice coming out hoarse. He cleared his throat.

"Yes." Richard picked up the tray and led the way.

When they all had a glass of champagne, they looked to him for a toast. His mind went blank.

"To your happiness," Meredith said, filling the tiny pause easily, her smile warm with happiness, her voice so sincere it made his eyes sting. She clinked glasses with her father and her friend, then turned to him.

Again her eyes implored. He stepped forward and drew a note from the crystal when he touched their glasses with his. "And a long life together," he proposed, then immediately wondered if that had been wise, considering their ages.

Meredith's smile assured him he'd done fine. He relaxed and enjoyed the champagne. The wedding was duly planned for Labor Day weekend, only four weeks away. The women discussed their clothing and the colors for the bouquets.

He had a sudden vision of Meredith in a white flowing dress, the green fire in her eyes hidden behind a gossamer veil until he lifted it for the traditional kiss. Hunger poured through him, and he experienced a great need to lay his claim on her by rushing her upstairs and making sweet tempestuous love to her at once.

He closed his eyes and pinched the bridge of his nose as if he had a headache. When he looked up, he met Genna's bright blue eyes. A flush spread up his neck. He almost thought she could see into his mind.

It wasn't long before the older couple stood to go. "Dinner was delicious," each of them complimented Meredith.

Sutter preened a bit. After all, he'd helped her learn all she knew about cooking. In fact, he'd taught her most of the things she knew about life.

At the door, he draped his arm across her shoulders after she'd kissed her father's cheek one last time He removed it self-consciously when he saw Richard observe that casual possessiveness. He met his friend's glance and returned it without flinching. Meredith went back into the apartment.

Richard shook his hand, accepted his congratulation once again and departed with his arm around his lady Sutter locked the door and went to find Meredith.

She was washing the champagne glasses. He picked up a towel and dried them. The domestic scene irritated him The events of the evening made him feel . . . unsettled.

"I'm so glad for them," Meredith rattled on. "The wedding will be lovely. Blue is Genna's color. Don't you think so?"

"I guess." He didn't want to think about it. Richard had asked him to be his best man.

All this talk about marriage . . . He glanced at Meredith, who was chatting away. He'd told her he never intended to marry. He hadn't seduced her with lies and love words. Hell, he hadn't done anything she hadn't wanted.

"Should the groom wear a white tux or maybe gray? That would look nice with his hair." She looked at him expectantly.

"I don't know," he said. "Look, do we have to talk about this anymore tonight?"

He saw at once he'd hurt her feelings. All emotion left her face, and her expression became carefully blank.

"Of course not." She chased the last bubbles down the sink and dried her hands. "There. All done. I think I'll go on up. I'm tired." She smiled, offered her mouth for a kiss then skipped out of the room, carrying that spoiled cat like a baby.

He flipped on the television and tried to shake off the nervy way he felt by listening to the world news. It was depressing as usual, but he didn't hear half of it. He kept seeing the velvet softness of Meredith's eyes when he'd snapped at her and the way she'd blinked and the way the glow had disappeared like a light switched off.

He rubbed his forehead where the tightness had grown into a full-blown headache. Why had she given him that look of entreaty earlier in the evening? Had she thought he would say something cutting to the other couple about marriage? Obviously she had.

Damn. She'd been happy until he'd told her he'd had enough wedding talk. He shouldn't have said that. He knew how she nattered on about something that pleased her.

He curled a hand into a fist and struck his thigh. He could have listened. It hadn't been necessary to snap at her. Not that he'd actually spoken harshly, but he'd made it plain he didn't care to hear any more about the damned marriage.

Leaping restlessly from the chair, he turned out the lights, checked the doors and went up the steps.

His room was empty.

He stared at the bed, which was still neatly made up. He went over and flung the covers off as if he expected her to be concealed under them somehow. No light in the bathroom. He returned to the hall and stared at the closed door across the way.

Stalking to it, he opened it with controlled anger. "What the hell are you doing in here?" he demanded.

She propped herself up on her elbow. T.C. peered over her shoulder.

"I thought you might want to be alone," she explained. "You seemed ... tired. Do you have a headache?"

"Yes," he snapped, striding across the room. He scooped her into his arms. "And it sure as hell won't be helped by wondering where you are and what you're up to all night!"

"Well, really, Sutter," she complained. "I was just thinking of you."

"Ha!" He dumped her on their bed and headed for the bathroom. After taking some aspirin and brushing his teeth, he shucked his clothes and headed for bed. T.C. was curled up on his pillow.

Sutter scooped the cat up and deposited him outside the door. He closed it quickly before the tomcat could run back in. A smile tugged at the corner of his mouth. The other time he'd tried to make love to Meredith with the damned cat in the room, T.C. had thought he was invited to the romp. He'd tried to crawl right in between them. Meredith had laughed and laughed, he remembered.

He turned toward her. She was lying back on the pillow, her eyes on him. He stopped by the bed, his body unfailing in its reaction to her. She glanced down, then back at his face.

"I'm not asking you to make love with me," he said gruffly, "just don't leave our bed because of hurt feelings."

"What did you expect me to do?"

He sat down and smoothed her hair off her temple. "I don't know." Tenderness stabbed at his heart, or whatever it was that ached inside his chest and aspirin couldn't touch. Her next words took him completely by surprise.

"I think I'd better go home. I can't stay here indefinitely, and we're obviously getting on each other's nerves. I guess I can live with a guard for a while."

It was like a kick in the chest. "No."

"Sutter—"

"Your father knows we're lovers," he heard himself say.

"Well, he's not exactly blind."

"I know." He couldn't keep from caressing her shoulder and letting his hand slip down to cup her breast, which reacted against his palm as if it had been waiting all evening for this.

When he saw her eyes on him, he flushed and removed his hand. Reaching for control he wasn't sure he had, he turned out the light and climbed into bed. On his side. Careful not to touch her.

After an eternity, he couldn't take any more. "I'm sorry," he said. "I didn't mean to hurt you."

She sniffed. "Will you kiss me?" she asked.

He couldn't get to her fast enough. He kissed her until the blood pounded in his brain like a freight train on loose rails. The fires of desire burned in him until he was white-hot. He couldn't get enough of her sweetness. He drank and drank at the well of her mouth. Finally, needing more, he slipped down her, leaving a trail of wet kisses along her middle, until he reached the sweet tender place of her desire.

He made love to her as he'd never done before, tasting her all over, until he knew every texture of her body. He took her to completion, then did it again, as if there would be no tomorrow. Finally he sank into her and sought his own pleasure until he'd exhausted every shred of passion he'd ever possessed.

And still he held her, their bodies joined, until long after she'd fallen asleep.

"Hold still now. There, it's all right. Oh, no..." Meredith closed her eyes as water flew all over the place. T.C. gave a pitiful cry, his gaze asking for mercy. She ruthlessly poured another cup of water over him. Before he could shake the excess off this time, she scooped him up into a towel and put him in her lap to dry off. She rubbed him until his fur stuck up in fluffy spikes.

"Spoiled cat," Sutter murmured, pausing at the door to watch.

She wrinkled her nose at him. "He has to have a monthly bath. I'm allergic to cat dander, and that's supposed to keep the dander down without drying out his skin."

"I suppose next you'll use conditioner on him."

She perked up. "Bright idea, Sutter. Cats lick their fur, so the conditioner would have to be edible. Say, I'll bet we could make a fortune in cat conditioner. We could use CNI facilities. Cat Network, Incorporated. How does that sound?" she teased.

After letting T.C. go—he'd hide under the bed until he got hungry or decided to trust her again—she wiped up the bathroom and hung the towels to dry. Then she wrapped her arms loosely around Sutter's waist and leaned against him.

He hesitated before bending to her mouth for their first kiss of the day, which was unusual, for the day was half gone.

They were wary around each other, she reflected. Sutter was right. They couldn't be friends and lovers at the same time. Instead of drawing closer, as she'd thought they'd do, they seemed hell-bent on moving farther apart.

With sudden clarity, she realized her love and her belief weren't enough. He had to feel the same. Unless he believed in their future, as she did, there would always be an element of uncertainty between them. It was too shaky a foundation for love to grow and bloom fully.

"Are you ready for lunch?" he asked, running his fingers through her hair, brushing out the droplets that T.C.'s shaking had deposited there.

"Yes."

"Let's go out."

She agreed and asked for ten minutes to change clothes
and freshen up. After changing into beige slacks and a
golden yellow peasant blouse, she rejoined Sutter in the
living room and they went to their favorite Mexican restaurant.

The place was popular, and they had to wait for a table.
They took a seat in the bar and had a fruit punch while
waiting. The television was tuned to a news program.

"Turning to local news: a kidnapping attempt was foiled
his morning by an employee of InnerSpace, an interior
design firm of Sacramento. The suspect tried to force the
owner of the company, Ms. Beryl West, into her car at
gunpoint. Fortunately, her scream attracted an archi-
tect...."

The camera focused on the scene, where police investi-
gators held back reporters with a band of yellow plastic
ribbon. Next the TV station showed a police drawing of
the suspect while the newscaster cautioned the listeners that
the man, who'd gotten away, was armed and considered
dangerous.

"My God," Sutter said, leaping from his chair.

Meredith gasped as recognition dawned on her. The
suspect was Larry Fisher. The resemblance to the photo
was unmistakable.

"Come on," Sutter ordered. He threw a bill on the table, and they left without waiting for change.

Outside, she spotted Barney casually leaning against the
fender of his car, reading the sports section of the paper.
Sutter pulled her along at a furious pace.

"Fisher made a move," he told the startled Barney when
they walked right up to him.

"In the restaurant?" Barney asked. He drew his gun, his
eyes sweeping the area.

"No. Not Meredith." Sutter's face was so set, his eyes so cold, she feared for the culprit if Sutter got his hands on him. "Let's go to the office. Have you talked to Ned this morning?" At Barney's nod, Sutter ordered, "Tell him to meet us there."

Meredith decided all the policemen in the city were working on the kidnapping case; otherwise, Sutter and Barney would have been arrested for speeding, reckless driving and a host of other crimes as they tore along the freeway to the headquarters of CNI. Ned was waiting for them.

"You must have come by jet," she remarked dryly. No one paid the slightest heed to her little joke.

Sutter led the way to his office. "How did Fisher get away?"

Ned scowled. "He didn't exit from the door he usually uses. We thought he was still in the warehouse."

Sutter used a very specific, very nasty expression Meredith had never heard him say. While the three men tried to figure out the troubled young man's strategy, Meredith sorted through a puzzle in her own mind.

Finally, she broke in. "I don't understand. Didn't you have any guards on the designer? I mean . . . why did you think he'd try to kidnap me and not her?"

She looked at Ned. He returned her gaze without speaking. Realizing Sutter made the decisions, she turned to him.

"It was in the note," he explained irritably. "Why he tried to take Beryl . . ." He shrugged. "Who knows what's in a madman's mind?"

"What note?" Meredith persisted. "I saw the one about the blonde. He knew I had dark hair. So does Beryl." Meredith brushed tendrils of hair behind her ears. She noticed her hands were trembling.

"The first note," Sutter said. "It said—"

He and Ned exchanged glances. The silence stretched until it became uncomfortable.

Ned cleared his throat. "Maybe we'd better look at the notes again," he suggested.

Sutter went to a picture on the wall and moved it aside. He spun the dial and opened a wall safe. From it, he removed a brown envelope. He returned to his desk and opened the flap. He withdrew all the threatening messages, the one directed to Linda, warning her about dating other men, and those to himself.

Meredith went and leaned over his shoulder. She read the one to Linda aloud. "Which was next?" she asked.

"This one." Sutter held it up.

Meredith read it to the group. "You took my woman, now I'll take yours." She read the third one about the blonde. Confused, she looked at Sutter. "Where's the one about me?"

He snorted in irritation. "This one." He held it up to her as if she were nearsighted.

"It doesn't say my name."

"Yes, it does," he stated. He read it again, then again.

"It wasn't me," she said slowly, incredulously.

"Of course it was you."

Ned spoke up. "Sutter and I made a list—"

"That's right," Sutter broke in. "It had to be you. I'd not seen another woman in months, not since you called me when Richard had his heart attack. It was you," he said adamantly, daring her to challenge him on this.

"No," she said.

Chapter Thirteen

"It was the newspaper. The article," Meredith clarified when the three men looked at her blankly. "You and the decorator at your town house, drinking wine in front of the fire. Who else would Fisher think you were interested in? It was clear you were lovers."

Some words were terribly hard to say, she discovered. *Lover* was one of them, especially when it applied to another woman in Sutter's life.

He glared at her, further enraged by her conclusion. "We were never lovers," he snapped. *"Never."*

"Well, it looked like it, and that's what Fisher went on... appearances. The same as anyone would," she added, hating herself for remembering and letting it hurt. "Anyway, I can go home. It's obvious he doesn't know about me."

"No." Sutter stood and jammed his hands into his pockets. "It's too dangerous. You might be next. We don't know—"

She turned away from him, and her eyes met the security chief's. Silent communication passed between them. He was a wise man, and he, too, recognized the truth.

"I'm going home," she reiterated.

Before Sutter could refuse again, Ned spoke up. "I think she's right. Fisher's actions today prove we were all wrong in our judgment of him."

Tension mounted when Sutter propped his fists on the desk and leaned on them, his scowl indicative of his fury. "And if we're wrong again?"

Meredith put her hand on his arm. She'd always remember his caresses, she thought, and the small tortured groans of passion he gave as he held himself back until she received all the pleasure he could give her. She'd remember the heated scent of their bodies blending in perfect unison and the taste of his mouth on hers, exciting her as nothing ever had . . . or would.

He'd always hold a special place in her heart, this strong, dynamic man. Friend, confidant, lover.

But she accepted that he would always be a solitary man. He'd share his body and his passion, but never his heart and his love. She couldn't live without them.

She released him. "I'll take my chances," she replied. She even managed to smile. "Barney, could I get a lift? I need to pack and get T.C."

Barney looked at Sutter, but Sutter was as silent as a stone. Finally he nodded and abruptly went to the window and looked outside, his back to the room.

"Sure," the guard said, standing.

Meredith went to the door, paused, then left without looking back. Barney followed her silently down the steps.

Outside, a noise from the guard booth attracted their attention.

A man with a gun stood there.

"Get down," Barney ordered, drawing his own weapon.

She ducked behind the security vehicle. Glancing up, she saw Sutter standing at his window as he'd been when she'd left. He said something over his shoulder, and Ned Barker appeared at the next window. She knew they understood the situation immediately when they saw Barney with his gun. They moved back from sight.

"Drop your weapon," Barney called when Larry Fisher stepped out of the guard shack.

Fisher whirled and ducked back inside. He reappeared, holding the groggy guard in front of him. "I want to see Kinnard," he said, "right now!"

"What for?" Barney asked.

Meredith looked at him in surprise. He sounded so casual.

"I want to talk to him. Come out from behind that van—the woman, too—or I'll kill him." He pushed the gun against the guard's temple.

Barney laid a hand on Meredith's shoulder. "Stay put." He called to Fisher. "Put your gun away, and we'll talk."

Meredith watched the action through the van's windows, ready to duck her head if necessary. Barney leaned nonchalantly on the vehicle, his gun hand resting on the short hood, ready to fire.

Fisher pushed the guard in front of him and crossed the parking lot to an alcove in the building. He squinted against the afternoon sun and peered at Meredith. "You're the one I saw at his house, not the other. He's here, isn't he?"

"Yeah," a quiet voice said.

Meredith nearly had a heart attack. Sutter came around the building from the front and confronted the madman.

Sutter glanced over at her. His eyes met hers, looking her over in a slow caress that startled her. He smiled slightly, then started on toward the alcove.

She thought her heart would burst in its terror for him. Through its frantic pounding, she could hear his steps on the pavement, the sound of Fisher's harsh breathing as he waited....

Without thinking, she ran. Straight into Sutter's arms.

He held her and rocked her, his embrace so tight she could scarcely breathe.

"Why did you come out? You were safe inside," she scolded, rubbing her hands over his warm flesh. She was afraid, so afraid.

"Go back to Barney," he murmured, his lips at her temple.

"No." She looked at him.

"Ned and I have a plan." Sutter kissed her eyes closed. He knew what the true darkness of hell looked like. It was in her eyes. His, too, probably.

He looked at Fisher over her head as she clung to him, then he pulled her hands off him and put her behind him. He was going to try to talk the troubled youth into laying down his weapon. If that failed, he was to lure the boy out of the alcove so Ned or Barney could get a clear shot at him.

The guard that Fisher held was an older man. He'd evidently been hit over the head with the end of the pistol. Fisher pushed the man aside, and he fell against the wall, cradling his head.

"You're the one I want," Fisher said, leveling the gun.

Sutter gave Meredith a push toward the security vehicle. "You got me," he said.

"You took my woman—"

"No, he didn't," Meredith said, stepping out and glaring at Fisher. "Linda didn't want you. You frightened her."

"Don't say that! She wanted me! She was... He interfered! Don't tell me she didn't want me!" He pointed the barrel at Meredith.

Sutter grabbed Meredith's shoulders and pushed her toward Barney. "Get the hell out of here and let me handle this!" he said, in a tone so fierce and low it was almost a growl.

She gave him a glance just as fierce, but did as she was told for once. When she was behind the van, Sutter faced the young man again. He felt sorry for the kid. Love, no matter what kind or how one-sided, could hurt like hell.

"Put your gun down," he ordered. "No one will hurt you as long as you do exactly what I say, I give you my word."

Fisher snorted and waved the gun wildly. "Your word, man? Your word?"

"My word," Sutter repeated. "You have one minute." He looked at his watch, then at the window above the alcove.

Fisher glanced up, his manner uncertain. "You don't fool me. There's no one up there. It's Saturday."

Thank God for small favors, Sutter thought. He tried to remember what Genna had told him in June in case they had a confrontation with Fisher at his aunt's house.

Keep him talking. Don't mention Linda. That would only increase the rage. Offer help. Let him see you're concerned. Tell him there are people who care.

"What did you want to see me about?" Sutter asked.

"You took my woman," Fisher accused.

Sutter ignored the remark. "There's a way out of this."

"I want to know where she is."

"There are people who know how to help you, people who care. I'll put you in touch with them."

"I can hit your woman from here."

A spasm of helplessness ran over Sutter. Why should this person, with his unhappy life, trust him?

"Larry," he said, trying to put them on a personal basis, "I know it's hard to believe, but there are good people in the world. I know. I found some of the best."

The very best. Forgive me, Meredith.

"Your woman loves you," Fisher said suddenly, as if that fact had just come to him. His dark eyes blazed with resentment and emotions Sutter could only guess at.

"Yes."

"She'd die for you."

"I know."

"No one's ever loved me like that."

Sutter couldn't afford to think about Meredith's love yet, and he wasn't sure how to respond to Larry's statement. The younger man's mood seemed to have changed. He no longer sounded angry, only matter-of-fact in a despairing sort of way.

Just one person's love could save a child....

Sutter realized he truly wanted to get help for this troubled, mixed-up young man.

"Linda didn't love me like that."

"She thought of you as a...friend," Sutter said, then changed the subject. "I know a doctor. A good one. She's treated people like you. She'll help you."

"No one will help me. I asked, a long time ago, but they left me with my aunt. She hated me. She said I was—" He wiped tears from his eyes. "She called me names."

Sutter quelled the useless anger at the woman who'd hurt this boy. Fisher's problems went deeper than that, but still...*one person...one person's love.* Could it have made a difference?

"We'll help you. You have my word."

Larry's mood changed again. The bereft boy disappeared. His mouth hardened, and he looked dangerous once more. "I don't care. I don't need her. I don't need anybody."

He took two steps toward Sutter. The barrel of the gun trembled, but the aim was steady. As Sutter watched, he realized Fisher was going to pull the trigger. The intent was in his eyes.

Sutter's muscles bunched in one desperate leap.

Meredith had watched and listened with a morbid fascination while Sutter and Fisher played out their tangled drama. She could see Ned Barker in the window above Fisher, his weapon ready if Fisher stepped out from the building only a few more feet.

Barney, too, was ready, but he couldn't do much with Sutter in the way. Meredith wondered how long Sutter could keep Fisher occupied. She noted that the young man's anger wasn't really directed at Sutter. It seemed to be more internal.

She prayed that Fisher would give up and put the gun down. Just then a flash of movement riveted her attention. Her heart plummeted to her feet. She watched as two bodies locked together in a deathlike embrace. She saw the gleam of the sun bouncing off the cool metal of the gun.

"No!" she cried. She started to run. Barney grabbed at her, but she fought him off.

She was halfway to the struggling bodies when she heard the shot. Sutter and Fisher stopped dead still like a frozen tableau, then they sank to the pavement.

"No." She ran toward them, her heart bursting.

* * *

Sutter laid the youth on the pavement and pushed the fallen gun out of reach. Taking his handkerchief out, he placed it on the chest wound. "An ambulance," he called, glancing over his shoulder at Barney.

Barney was already on the van's phone. Ned Barker, the security chief, appeared with two other guards. He ordered one to the front gate and the other to tend the older guard, who was still in the alcove holding his head.

"You all right?" Ned asked Sutter.

Sutter nodded. He checked Fisher's pulse. "He didn't intend to hurt me. I realized he was going to shoot himself and tried to stop him." He frowned and looked at the wound, evidence of his failure.

The ambulance and police arrived at the same time. For a few minutes, confusion reigned, but the police detective soon had the witnesses and details of the case sorted out. Sutter stood and moved away when the paramedic stooped by Fisher and took over. He looked around.

He saw Meredith standing quietly to one side, her arms crossed in front of her. She rubbed her upper arms as if she were cold. Then he noticed the tremors running through her.

He walked over and pulled her into his arms, holding her close, reveling in the warmth of her, the scent of her, the incredible miracle of her sweet womanliness. He longed to absorb her fright and remove it from her.

"I'd give anything," he murmured into her hair, "to have spared you this."

She cried then. Not a silent weeping of tears, but great huge sobs that shook her from head to toe. It frightened him almost as much as when she'd run to him in the face of that gun.

"Meredith," he whispered, trying to comfort her. "Meredith, it's all right now. It's over."

She pulled back from his crushing embrace. "You could have been killed," she said. "You could have been *killed.*"

The detective interrupted them, asking questions, getting their names and addresses, the name of the officer who'd worked with them on the Fisher case.

"The Fisher case," she repeated, and watched as the medics lifted the young man into the ambulance. Sutter knew what she was thinking. Larry Fisher would be a one-day headline in the papers, then he'd become just another statistic in a crime report.

Another life wasted.

But maybe not. With proper help, the boy might be saved.

Sutter turned to Meredith. She was standing utterly still, watching the action around her as if she were invisible. He was worried about her.

"Do you need us anymore?" he asked the detective.

"No. You're free to leave."

Sutter put his arm around Meredith. "Come on, brat. Let's go home."

She stared at him, her lashes wet and spiked from her tears. "You haven't called me that in years."

"I know." The terrible, aching tenderness for her washed over him. He wanted to wrap himself around her and shield her from the elements like a robin with one egg.

To his surprise, she went to the van and started to climb in. He hauled her out and led her to his car, his arm clamped tightly around her waist.

When they were on the road, she stared at the traffic in front of them. It was a few minutes before she spoke. "I want to go home. To my home."

"No."

"Yes."

"We'll talk about it." He knew he couldn't leave her alone. He reached out and touched her hand. Cold as an ice cube. She was in shock. He knew it even if she didn't. Also he had a thing or two to say to her about throwing herself into danger.

The sight of her running to him! It had scared the hell out of him. Emotion, greater than he'd ever known, welled up in him. He couldn't put a name to it, but it was black as death, hot as a blast furnace and pure as the basic elements.

He was going to pound a few grains of sense into her head if it was the last thing he did. Right after he made love to her.

A handy grove of trees tempted him, but he kept driving, his eyes on the road, his hands clenched on the steering wheel to keep from reaching for her. He made the turn onto his street, up the drive, into the garage. Home. Blessed home.

He leaped from the car and came around to her before she could open her door. "Out," he said. When she didn't move fast enough, he helped her with hands under her arms, snatching her to him and carrying her into the house. Straight to the bedroom.

When he put her down, she stood there, her face as pale as carved stone. Alarm rippled along his veins. She was so quiet. Too quiet.

"Meredith?" he questioned softly.

"What?" She sounded as lifeless as a computer voice.

Sutter ran his hands over her. The tremors had stopped, but she was still as cold as an ice sculpture. He trampled his need of her, the demanding urge to have her beneath him, her body accepting his in the ages-old celebration of life over death.

"Let's get these off," he said. He undressed her, then himself, and guided her into the bathroom. There, he turned the shower on full and hot. Lifting her, he stepped into the stream and let the water rush over them.

She closed her eyes and rested her head against the tiles. He kissed her pale lips. When she turned her head, he soaped his hands and began washing her, taking his time, feeling the heat from the water gradually warm her. It wasn't until the water began to cool that he let her out.

After rubbing her with a giant towel, he wrapped it around her, dried himself and carried her to their bed. He put her nightshirt on her and tucked her under the covers.

"I'm not sick," she said.

"You've had a shock. Rest now."

He sat beside her and rubbed her hair with a towel until she went to sleep. An occasional tremor shook her body even then. With a touch on her forehead, he left her and went to the kitchen to put on a pot of coffee. He remembered they'd never gotten around to lunch, and it was almost time for dinner.

T.C. rubbed against his legs. Sutter studied the cat, then picked it up and stroked the black fur. The cat gazed back at him, then gave a soft, questioning meow.

"She'll be okay," Sutter said.

His throat closed then, and he put his free hand over his face. For all his efforts, he'd failed to protect Meredith from danger.

Meredith woke slowly to the silken caress of Sutter's hand on her. She knew it was him before she opened her eyes. With a struggle, she lifted her lashes and gazed at him.

"Awake at last," he said. He was lying beside her, raised on an elbow while he gently explored her body.

Her earlier fears returned as she remembered the danger he'd been in. She wrapped both arms around him and buried her face against his chest.

After a minute, that wasn't enough. She wanted him inside her. Desire and despair commingled as she began caressing him.

"Rest," he advised, worry in his eyes.

She shook her head. "I want you. Now."

He groaned and pulled her close, his hands running over her back and hips, cupping her to him. "I want you, too. It's been hell watching you sleep."

She felt him against her, his body rigid with passion, ready to take her. His hands slipped between them and discovered she was ready. He kissed her first, a long, drowning kiss of tormented need that matched her own.

Rising, he moved over her and came into her. She clung to him in welcome.

Looking into her eyes, he made love to her, each thrust gentle but bold, carrying her to forgetfulness. The terror of the past hours receded, replaced by his touch, his murmurs of encouragement and his passionate longing.

He brought her to the edge of bliss and let her waft down, then he brought her to the precipice again.

"Now," she whispered.

Together they went over the falls.

Later, when their hearts beat with a normal rhythm, and their breathing was no longer ragged gasps, she spoke what had been in her mind since the revelations in his office concerning the notes.

"You love me," she said.

"Yes," he admitted. "For what it's worth, I do."

Chapter Fourteen

With a grim countenance, Sutter dressed. At the bedroom door he paused. "We're out of milk. I'll go to the store."

Meredith listened to him leave. He didn't take his car. Getting up, she went to the window and watched him walk down the pavement. Evening was nigh, and the sky glowed with mysterious lights and shadows as the sun set behind a bank of clouds.

She sat in the easy chair and stared into space, not doing anything, while sadness consumed her. Her mind roamed through the past and the days of her youth when she'd spun such daydreams—all of them centered on Sutter. Then she considered the events of that turbulent day.

The irony of Fisher going after the designer while Sutter guarded the wrong woman almost drew a smile. Such is life, she reflected with a poignancy that tore at her control. One had to take the bitter with the sweet.

The sweetness resulted from the hours she'd spent in his company and in his arms and from the fact that his every thought had been for her safety. Well, maybe not every thought...

The bitterness returned to her in a rush, born in that moment in Sutter's office when she'd realized Fisher had never mentioned her in his notes, not once. Ned had known it all along. Only Sutter had assumed *your woman* had meant Meredith.

She sighed shakily, recalling all the truths that had hit her at that moment. The first one had been that Sutter truly thought of her as his woman. The second was that he must love her, not just as a friend, but the way a man loves a woman, just as she'd thought. The hardest truth had followed: he would never permit that love to grow and develop.

Why, Sutter?

Because his loving others hadn't made a damn bit of difference in his life.

She'd thought to show him how wonderful it could be, living together. And there had been moments of happiness between them. But that wasn't enough, either. She wanted a lifetime, and Sutter would never believe in love enough to build a future for them.

If he didn't trust his own feelings toward her, then it stood to reason he'd never trust her love for him.

The knowledge dropped like a stone into her soul, shattering dreams she'd harbored for years. Sutter, with so much love in him, would never share it, not with her. If she battered her heart much longer against the icy wall encasing his, it would break into pieces so small she might never get them together again.

Sutter put the milk away and stood for a moment in the dark kitchen. T.C. rubbed against his legs and ran to his empty bowl. Sutter fed the cat and trod silently up the stairs. An hour of walking hadn't resolved the turmoil in his mind.

He still couldn't figure out why Meredith had become so upset in his office when she found out her name hadn't been mentioned in the threats. So what? Sooner or later, his association with her would have led Fisher to the right woman.

Which was exactly what had happened, he recalled. By taking her into his home, by staying constantly with her, he'd told the world she was his. By taking her to the office with him to consult with his security chief, he'd led her into the path of a madman.

She'd been afraid for him. He'd seen that. She also loved him. So why had she decided to leave?

He opened the bedroom door and went in. The room was dark, and his heart pounded suddenly, the only thing he could hear in the silence. He started out, intent on searching for her, when he spotted her in the chair. He flicked on a lamp.

Cautiously, afraid he'd startle her, he walked forward until he could see her face. She stared out the window. He moved in front of it. She looked at him.

''Meredith?''

Meredith heard him from a distance. She lifted her gaze to his. Like in a dream, she remembered that in a few short days, he'd given her ecstasy and tenderness and passion such as she'd never dreamed existed. Why couldn't things last? Why couldn't they stay the same?

With infinite regret, she rejected that idea. She wanted more. Sutter wanted less. It was time to wake up. Someday she'd look back on all this and laugh. Someday.

She roused herself to ask, ''Have a nice walk?'' She even managed to smile.

"Yeah." Sutter wasn't sure how to approach her. She looked so...distant. "Meredith?" he questioned in the gentlest voice.

"It's okay," she said. "*I'm* okay."

His chest felt like a burning lump of coal. To look into her eyes was to look into darkness. She thought she was all right. He knew she wasn't. She'd fallen into the heart of error that morning, and she wasn't out yet. It was still there, in her eyes, and it was his fault. He had to reach her.

"No," he said. "You're not okay."

Meredith wondered why, if the English language had over a half-million words, she couldn't think of a few to say.

Sutter dropped to his haunches beside her and took her hand. "Are you still upset because of today? I'll take care of things. That boy will get the help he needs, I promise."

"I know," she said. Unable to keep herself from touching him, she caressed his cheek and rested her hand there for a second before removing it. A sigh escaped her.

"Ned knew," Sutter said. "He knew all the time."

She gave him a questioning glance. No wonder. He wasn't making sense. "When we got the note, he said we had to figure out who the woman was. I knew who she was. You."

"I know all that." She brushed a hand over her eyes. "Do we have to talk about it right now?"

He remembered saying something similar to her about her father's wedding. She'd grown so quiet that time. She'd left his bed and he'd had to fetch her back.

The glow, he thought. He wanted the glow in her eyes...the way she looked when he made love to her, her gaze all hot and wide open with love...then the glow, melting over him like lava before she squeezed her eyes shut against the powerful pleasure they shared.

There was only one way he could think to reach her, to bring her back from that silent abyss. He'd only said the words once, tonight, just before he left. Now he had to make her believe them.

"Don't close me out," he murmured.

Meredith swallowed hard. She'd thought she was beyond emotion now that she'd accepted the truth about her future, or lack of one, with Sutter. But looking at him . . .

His eyes—dark blue, black-lashed, sexy, tender, gentle—narrowed as she gazed at him, and she saw worry in them.

She didn't know how to dissemble, so she stated her plans. "I'll leave in the morning. I'll pack first thing and be out before noon."

He surged to his feet, paced to the window, turned and rammed his hands into his pockets. "No."

"Sutter—"

"You said a year. By my estimation, we have about fifty weeks to go."

She closed her eyes briefly against pain, then forced herself to look at him. "It isn't enough."

He turned and stared out the window. With his back to her, he asked, "What isn't? Me? Us? What do you want?" He sounded tired, defeated.

She clamped her teeth into her lower lip when it trembled, and waited until she'd regained control. "I received the job offer from the National Park Service. They want me to help prepare a water study of all the parks in the western United States."

He whirled. A blood vessel throbbed so hard in his neck, she feared it might burst. "So. That's it, then. All your talk of love, all the times we made love and you cried out about loving me, it was . . . pillow talk. Now you've decided to leave."

She leaped to her feet. "No! I do love you. That isn't the problem."

"Then what the hell is?"

He spoke with such a quiet intensity, she almost went to him, but if she did, she knew she wouldn't be able to leave. It would be better if she did, for her and for him.

"If you're free of me," she began, "you might meet someone, someday, who can reach your heart."

"So help me, Meredith, you make less sense than a squawking chicken." He raked a hand through his hair. "Why don't you admit the real problem—you're tired of being with me."

"I'm not!" She lowered her voice. "But Sutter, think. If you ever meet a woman who gains your whole love...well, she'll be lucky, the one who shares to the fullest that deep passionate love I know you have inside."

"And what about my love for *you?*"

She pressed her fingers against her throbbing temples and drew a deep breath, slowly, for it hurt even to breathe.

"I do think you love me. On some level. In some way I haven't figured out yet. But obviously it's not enough to overcome your distrust of love. I know it's never worked for you...."

Her voice trailed away as he stalked toward her, his gaze as intent as a savage bent on destruction.

"Don't tell me how I love you," he uttered in a low tone that was almost a feral growl. He jerked her into his arms, holding her so close she couldn't tell if it was his heart or hers she felt beating so hard and fast. "Don't tell me how much or how little or on what level." He had never felt so frustrated. "They're not enough," he muttered. "The words aren't enough."

She touched him, soothing him. "Sutter, what's wrong?" she asked, looking perplexed and concerned.

He didn't want her pity. "I love you. It isn't enough, ei
ther, but it's all I have."

Her mouth parted, and he had to fight to keep from
bending his head to hers and taking that sweet nectar. H
wanted her. He wanted her like hell. With an ache in th
heart and a fever in the blood. How could he tell her al
that and sound like a sane man when he was going craz
with wanting her?

"I don't understand." She sounded uncertain. He'
done that to her.

"Dammit, I love you with everything that's in me. Wit
every breath I breathe. With every moment of every day
I've worried over you for years, and wanted you for ever
damn one of them. Don't tell me about love. I know abou
it."

"Yes, I know," she whispered, running her hands ove
his broad shoulders before gently moving away from him
"For you, it's been a hurting thing, a disappointment. Yo
told me. It never worked for you."

"That's right. When I was a kid, love never solved on
wrong thing in my life. But I'm a man now."

Meredith pressed her shaking lips together. She wasn'
sure what he was saying, what the message was in his eyes.

"Maybe love doesn't count for very much in this world
My love certainly never seemed to make a tinker's dam
worth of difference. But that's all you seem to want from
me . . . all you ever wanted from me. I'd decided to give i
a try. You said you wanted a year with me as your lover.
thought that would be enough time to see if we could worl
things out between us. Now you want to leave."

"I don't," she denied softly, hopelessly loving him. "
just thought . . . I mean . . ." She closed her eyes as the stu
pid tears jetted into them.

"Tell me how to make you happy."

She was wary. "You said sex was all there was."

He didn't answer.

"You said I lived in a fairy tale."

"Let me live there with you." He'd beg if he had to.

The hunger came from deep within him, welling up, growing larger with each breath until it filled his entire body. He felt as if he were coming apart. It was like an iceberg breaking up in his chest. There was pain. There was fear. He hadn't been so vulnerable for years.

"Meredith, love me."

Meredith heard his voice from a long way off, although he stood close to her. Hot kisses landed on her chin, her neck, when he took her into his arms again. She clung to him. "I do," she whispered. "Dear God, I have for most of my life."

"That's what I realized when I was walking," he told her, his mouth pasting love tokens, little sucking kisses, all over her face. "Just as I've loved you."

"Don't lie."

"I'm not. I admired you and your father. I saw the way both of you felt toward a woman I'd never met, but wish I'd known. She must have been a wise woman to raise a daughter like you." He spoke faster, with an edge of desperation. "You've grown into a beautiful woman, Meredith. One who isn't afraid to love. One who believes with all her loyal, honest, trusting heart that love can conquer every problem. Make me believe, too."

She wanted to. Heaven knew she wanted to. "You're wrong. I *am* afraid. I want all your love, right down to the secret cache you keep locked away, but not as a debt."

"Debt?"

"You think you owe me for putting me in danger, so you're going to pay me back by loving me."

"No," he denied, his voice dropping to a husky register.

"If we stay together," she warned, "I won't let you keep part of yourself hidden away so it won't be hurt when life gets rough. Do you understand?"

Sutter hesitated, realizing what she wanted, not sure if he could give it, nor what it was worth if he did.

Meredith drew a steadying breath and fought the tears as she waged a battle for Sutter's complete love. It was now or never. "You don't think your love is worth much. I do. I want it for me and for our children."

"You got it. All of it." His lips turned up in a sardonic smile. He was still skeptical, she saw, but maybe, maybe there was a chance for them after all.

"I want a marriage, a family and a house in the country with a swing set," she warned him.

"We'll look around for one," he promised, his hands roaming her back, caressing her waist, and doing other wild things to her. "In the meantime, we can paint this place... something brighter."

She was fast losing her ability to think. When he lifted her into his arms, she forgot all her resolutions and doubts.

He chose to sit in the chair and hold her in his lap. His body was fully aroused, ready for her. She wanted him the same way, with that sweet wildness singing through her heart.

"I've been a fool," he whispered, sliding his hands under her nightshirt. "My love never seemed to matter much but to doubt yours... that was stupid."

"Your love *does* matter."

"Will it be enough for the rest of our lives?"

"We've already shared eleven years," she reminded him.

"Eleven years," he repeated.

The vibrant heat of his voice warmed a hearthstone deep within her. A blaze grew in his eyes. The world seemed brighter all at once.

"If we've loved each other eleven years," he murmured, "then we should be able to make it another eleven."

"Easily."

"And if we make it twenty-two years, then we should be able to last another twenty-two. If we make it forty-four years—"

"We can make it another forty-four," she finished. She smiled at him.

He kissed her.

The earth shifted as he scooped her up and headed for the bed. He tossed off her nightgown and threw off his clothes. Then he made love to her as he had before, but there was a difference.

When she looked into his eyes, she knew what it was.

"It's gone," she said. She touched a finger to each of his beautiful blue eyes. "The darkness. The cold, secret darkness."

"It melted."

She gazed deeply into his eyes. A promise was given and received. She smiled, accepting his word.

Epilogue

Sutter removed the paintbrush from Meredith's hand and dropped it in a bucket of water. "Enough. I'll finish."

She smiled at him, then placed her hands in the small of her back and stretched the tired muscles. "You look cute as a speckled pup," she told him, grinning at the paint splatters on his face.

"Thanks." He finished the wall, then the last window sill, and washed out the roller and brushes. "We could have hired someone to do this," he said.

She'd insisted that they do the inside work. The house was decorated in shades of blue, brick red and warm beige. Plants and bright prints added color to every room...a sixteen of them.

"But it's more fun doing it ourselves."

"Fun," he repeated grumpily. "Thank heavens this is the last room." But he smiled.

It *was* fun, but then anything he did with her was heaven. They'd searched for five years before finding this sturdy old house on a small ranch outside Sacramento. From it, a person could see the snowy Sierras on most days. Cows grazed in the meadows and horses sniffed the spring air and frolicked in the paddocks.

"I'm going to hang my rainy-night picture over the hearth in here," she told him. "It seems to go with a den. You know, a quiet night indoors, reading or gazing into the fire."

"Like the invisible people in the houses."

"Yes." She was silent a moment. "I wonder how the folks are doing?"

He folded her into his arms, hearing the real question behind the spoken one. She was thinking of Travis, their four-year-old son, and missing him like crazy. He did, too.

Richard and Genna, the California grandparents, had taken him on a trip with them. They were going to stop in Alabama and let the kid visit with the other grandparents. They'd already been to see the Florida grandparents.

"They seemed to be having a good time when they called last night," he answered. Things were better with his father. At Meredith's urging, he'd talked to his stepmother, and together they'd confronted his father, who'd entered a therapy program to learn useful ways to control his rage.

"I wonder if Travis remembered who everyone was?"

"Stop worrying. He had them down pat from the pictures you showed him every night for the past month." He tried to keep a straight face.

"Are you laughing at me?" she demanded.

"No. Well, a little." He nuzzled her nose with his. "Let's take a shower."

She opened her eyes wide in shock. "You don't mean . . . you surely don't mean . . . *together?*"

"Is there another way?" he murmured.

He lifted her and carried her through the house to the master bath. There, he removed her old paint clothes, then his own. In the shower, he laid his hand flat on her abdomen.

"Anything you'd like to tell me?" he asked.

She wrinkled her nose at him. "You always know everything."

"How far?"

"Two months."

"A girl this time," he ordered.

"Maybe. Maybe not. We might have to try again." She laughed at his grimace.

"The first time scared me senseless. How much torture can a man take?"

"As much as a woman can," she assured him, not at all sympathetic. "Hurry," she suddenly said.

He looked into her eyes and saw her need. He hurried. After they'd bathed and dried off, he took her hand and led her to their bed. There, he made sweet, tempestuous love to her. It seemed to get better all the time. Not just their lovemaking, either, but everything . . . all of life.

Emotion rose to his throat, filling his chest with painful pleasure. He kissed her eyes closed. The glow was there, dazzling him, and he couldn't look at it for a moment. The feeling was too great.

Inside, he felt one sharp tearing pain, a reminder of the icy prison that had once enclosed his heart. He was free of the past, but he remembered it. Whenever he read a report on Larry Fisher's progress, he could only feel pity. *One person's love . . .*

In living with Meredith, Sutter had discovered a simple irrefutable truth, something he'd dimly realized when he'd confronted that pathetic, mixed-up kid five years ago.

His love *alone* hadn't been able to change anything, **but** *two* people, working together, could change the future. The love of a man and a woman—that was enough to change a lifetime.

What was so hard about that?

* * * * *

BIG SUMMER READ

Summer Reading At Its Best

In July, Harlequin and Silhouette bring readers the Big Summer Read Program. Heat up your summer with these four exciting new novels by top Harlequin and Silhouette authors.

SOMEWHERE IN TIME by Barbara Bretton
YESTERDAY COMES TOMORROW by Rebecca Flanders
A DAY IN APRIL by Mary Lynn Baxter
LOVE CHILD by Patricia Coughlin

From time travel to fame and fortune, this program offers something for everyone.

Available at your favorite retail outlet.

BSR